The Last Of The Virgins

George Che Atanga

T0114684

Langaa Research & Publishing CIG
Mankon, Bamenda

Publisher:
Langaa RPCIG
Langaa Research & Publishing Common Initiative Group
P.O. Box 902 Mankon
Bamenda
North West Region
Cameroon
Langaagrp@gmail.com
www.langaa-rpcig.net

Distributed in and outside N. America by African Books Collective
orders@africanbookscollective.com
www.africanbookscollective.com

ISBN: 9956-792-43-8

DISCLAIMER
All views expressed in this publication are those of the author and do
not necessarily reflect the views of Langaa RPCIG.

Dedication

To Feseh, my former fiancee and to my daughter

Preface

Since the first appearance of this short story, my readers have continually been accosting me on the way, either asking me a few questions or simply reproaching me on certain abnormalities. I have had questions like: why is your main character a girl instead of a boy? Why is she a virgin? Why choose Our Lady of Lourdes Secondary School? Why did you choose real names of places? Is the work fiction at all? Are you sure you have not written on a particular individual who is existing? Why is Evelyn punished in the end? Why should Lesley die at the end? Why do I refuse Evelyn from enjoying her beloved and worst of all, why is the work tense and tragic? Some have simply asked me why the work is so short while others have found the end of the work too abrupt and wish to know if I intend to continue it sometime.

I must say, I am most enchanted with the concern my readers have shown in the work which at the beginning I thought was going to be a child's play and to be forgotten the moment the reader finishes reading. These questions are exactly those which would encourage me to work harder. To answer the numerous questions above, I would say, that's just what inspired me to write. What interests people is the abnormality in life. Many people would like to read about the woman in Bamenda who got married to two husbands and treated them as her wives by keeping them in her own house to work for her and owe allegiance to her. Likewise, many people would like to read about the 9'year-old girl who has put to bed twice in Buea and is married to an 85 year old chief but few persons would care to know about Mr. Peter Ambe who was born at the correct time, got married to two wives, had 7 children and died at the age of 70. Late in 1983, I met an Israeli friend in Germany and he wanted to know where Cameroon could be located in the globe. I tried in vain to give him a geographical location. Then he asked me in what field Cameroon was noted in. I replied that it was noted for peace, that there was religious freedom, that the Cameroonian accepted every condition offered to him good or bad, that day dawn was mostly at 6 am and nightfall at 6pm, that we had rainy and dry seasons. 'Boring country", he said. He had read about Uganda and its president - Idi Amin who was a cannibal. He had read about South Africa which makes headlines of news in every TV station in the world and about Ethiopia with its excessive drought and famine, Five months later, he came and told me that he had known about Cameroon, not from any studies but because there was an abnormality in Cameroon; an attempted military take-over.

To sum up what I have been saying; what has inspired me to write and what has urged you to read on and on has been the abnormality or in other words you have been searching for the normality. In short, it is the unexpected which makes the core of my works.

Again I would emphasize that despite the apparent reality in the work, no character nor the narration is real. Every single incident in the work is imaginary and the whole work is pure fiction.

My thanks go first to the whole team of NUSANG BOOKS for digging up this manuscript for republication, to Mr. Jeti Menget for proofreading the work and to the whole (PPA) Palace Production Association for their literary activities on my works which have helped to put me on my literary path.

George Che ATANGA
Bamenda

Chapter 1

I was born in a small quarter in Bafut called Niko, My
father was a cook to a certain British missionary who
worked in Bafut during the Late 50s and early 60s. When
he retired in 1961 and went home; my father was forced to
remain jobless for some years during which land my six
younger sisters and brothers suffered exceedingly, living in
great penury.

My father, not being interested in leaving us to go out of
Bafut for a job, tried his hand at farming. He cultivated coffee
and his plantation yielded him some profit. With this, I was
able to go to the primary school at the age of 7 which was
considered tender those days, instead of 9, 10 or even 11.

After having repeated Infants One because I was
considered too young to go to the next class, I did eight years
before I could have my First School Leaving Certificate. I
could not proceed directly into the secondary school due to
no money even though I passed the Common Entrance
Examination which was an exceedingly rare phenomenon
reserved only to those of a considerably high aptitude. I was
then constrained to spend a miserable and gloomy year out of
school after which I tried the Common Entrance
Examination again the following year and passed so well that
I was awarded a government scholarship to enter Our Lady
of Lourdes Secondary School in Mankon, Bamenda.

I entered the secondary school at the age of 15 just when
I had undergone my maturity. I was strikingly beautiful,
ebony black in complexion with thick and dark eye-lashes. I
had the most beautiful hair in my school; thick, long and
neatly kempt, a beauty I attributed to the untiring care of my

dear mother. Unfortunately, I was forced to cut it down as the regulations of the school were suddenly revised by a new principal who had just arrived from Britain, a woman of about 50, an overzealous advocate of morality and conformism. Her reason was not that it consumed precious school time caring for it but that it attracted boys.

I would have been wanting very much in school, material-wise if not, thanks to the stringent school regulations, we were not permitted to wear any dress out of the school uniforms which were routinely changed. No one could thus detect that I was from a poor family since I had just my basic necessities, which kept me at the margin.

I studied veraciously and passed my examinations with good credits at the end of every term. Being from a staunch Christian family, since my father's master was a missionary of the Basel Mission, I lived in a close religious circuit and was wonderfully naive as to what concerned the social field. Worst of all, my mother had taught me that there were human devils haunting the earth in the form of boys and that keeping every boy out of one's way was keeping away the devil. I thus nursed a great fear for boys and still with a teenager's mind, l exaggerated the admonition so much such that it was later to produce serious consequences on my future.

I treated every male being with great suspicion. Whatever service a boy proposed to render to me was blatantly rejected. I remember one day after vacation, I struggled to get a vehicle at the Mankon Motor park to go home but the students being so many to journey to different directions and the vehicles too few, I was not lucky to journey. Many schools had closed on the same day and most of the vehicles chose to run the long distances like Yaoundé, Douala and Buea for it would give them a heavier purse. I was with a friend, a Wum girl who was my classmate. She was with her cousin who was a trader in town and he did all he could to help us have a vehicle but all in vain. When every possibility faded away and he found that we only had to spend the night in town and go the next day, he proposed to lodge us for the night in his one bedroom lodging.

My parents had warned me against spending the night in town. On top of it all, I had no responsible relation who could lodge me in town and this boy's invitation to spend the night in his one bedroom house looked dead suspicious. I turned down the invitation very bluntly despite the coaxes of my friend. They assured me that I would not get a vehicle and l promised them that I would spend the night with my parents even if it meant waiting late at the motor park. They bid me farewell and went their way. I continued my struggle and never gave a thought to what would happen if I did not get a vehicle.

Soon the sun was making its imperturbable descent behind the horizon and the cars started disappearing from the lorry park and never to come back. Darkness was rushing in fast and students who had got no occasion to journey were either to spend the night in their friends' houses or with their relatives who lived in town. I could not think of any and even if I did, I would not be able to get him or her for I never even knew much about the town. It looked like certain vagrants and even urchins had discovered that I was a stranded girl and were ready to pounce on me. Within a few minutes under the darkness, I was surrounded by undetectable and horrific faces and even though I cared very much for my portmanteau box which could be grabbed away; I soon found myself faced with the choice between caring for my own proper self which was tampered with by lawless and curious fingers or caring for my luggage and I inevitably chose, the former which was quite human. I was seriously rough handled and when I soon felt fingers penetrating, forbidden parts of my body, I seized my box and changed places still hoping that a late vehicle would come and pick me home.

The next spot I chose was a worse one for there was a flicker of light from an off-licence bar that fell on me and I could be detected from every direction. I thought that it was better because they would be scared by the light. This was 'true but I had only thrown off the lions to choose the tigers. It was the turn of drunkards to pounce on me. I was surrounded in less than a minute by ugly smelling drunkards who made interminable invitations for me to come in for a beer. They smelt ugly with beer and at each refusal I was physically molested. I was dragged up, here and there and finding that I risked very serious consequences if I insisted on going home, seized my box, tore myself off the crowd and made for the town but not knowing where I was going to exactly. Only then did I so much regret having rejected my friend's cousin's offer. Curious heads popped out from the darkness as I passed to get a better view of my face and some stopped me by blocking my way but I averted them and went on.

A taxi cleared in front of me and the driver told me to come in and when I told him that I had not got money, he proposed giving me a free lift. I still refused the invitation and he cursed and left. I was moving on and on without a set destination. I soon asked myself where I was going to while turning down invitations in this manner. At the same time two men were multiplying their steps behind me and I could not walk any faster due to the weight of my box. At the same time a private vehicle halted just ahead of me at the side of the road and gave me the opportunity to dodge the pursuers by going between them and the bank of the road. Just when I was about to pass the door opened violently and blocked the way. I was taken by awe as I found myself face to face with a white face, a woman for that matter. When the voice spoke, I recognized the voice of my principal. I breathed fresh air as she took me in her vehicle back to her house after she had learnt of all my troubles. She had suspected that some of us would get stranded and had come round for checkup.

The next morning I had no trouble in getting a car to go home. My parents bad waited for me the previous day and when I could not come, they bad feared what might have happened and when I narrated my story to them, they look me to a prayer group and we prayed the whole evening, thanking God for having saved me from the hands of the devils.

Chapter 2

As the school years passed on, I was getting more and more charming and more a mathematical problem, to boys who wanted to solve me. I turned down every approach nonchalantly and anyone who dared insist was sure to become my antagonist. The very first one had made his very bold attempt when I went home for vacation during my first year in school. This boy had been my classmate in the final class of the primary school but had gone to the Cameroon Protestant College the year before. He was thus making his second form in this college.

I was returning from Church and, worst of all, I had read the first lesson which came from the scriptures of Saint John. When I by passed "this thing" as I was afterwards to qualify him, he was standing with a group of boys. He greeted me very warmly and congratulated me for the fluency with which I read the Bible in the Church. I thanked him and passed away. He hurriedly ended his conversation with his colleagues and closed up behind me. When I turned and saw him coming, I was taken by a sudden fright and I also increased my speed. He nevertheless caught up with me and was already moving side by side with me. He whispered. I was evenly increasing my speed of walking. In fact, I was almost skipping when he attempted to hold my hand to slow me down. With all my might, I seized my hand from him and sent him staggering across the path.

Thank God, my parents were involved in a Sunday meeting which held them back or else they would have seen me, with this bastard and who would have convinced my hard-hearted mother that I had not anything doing with him.

He let loose an uneasy smile and asked me why I should be so boisterous. I told him that if only he knew what he was doing, he would realize its consequences. He was still walking abreast with me but I halted, made an about turn and gave him my back. I asked him to disappear from my side and threatened returning to the Church to report to my parents or shout for help if he did not leave me in peace. This by no means shook the stubborn lover who resorted to lavishing me with love poetry which I reckoned must have been carefully reproduced from a romantic novel written by a rustic and brokenhearted author. I stood still and he profited from this opportunity to empty his mind to me, telling me how he had long sought for such an opportunity to tell me how much he felt if I were to become his friend, we would bathe in an eternal pool of happiness.

I turned my face and perceived the bold wretch and hated him the more he babbled his poetry. When I concentrated my look, I nevertheless was convinced that the boy was attractive, or the same height and age with me. He was light in complexion with red and charming lips wearing a very beautiful favoris. He had an immaculate white shirt and a neat black trouser, an attire which was very rare those days, in fact, reserved to children of civil servants. I was afterwards to understand that it was their school occasional uniform. I also noticed that he spoke intelligently and commanded some eloquence.

"What is wrong in being in love? Is the popular slang in the world today not love and peace? Don't you find it out of place to hate me just because I love you? Tell me how you would behave if I meet you and start nagging, provoking and even assaulting you. Would there be any difference in your reaction? Peace and war to you seem to be alike."

I shivered under the weight of these energetic questions and was about to congratulate him for possessing such a high IQ when I realized myself and only said,

"I don't need your love. My father and my mother love me. God loves me too." He was about to say something when I sighed and made another threat to shout for help if he persisted. He was by no means scared by this threat and looked at both ends, obtained his excuse and made off.

I took the opposite direction and went home apparently satisfied but a little disturbed. 1 nursed a bitter hatred for this boy but a low voice in me was constantly asking me what this poor boy had done to deserve such hatred. He had only informed me that he loved me. What sense was there in detesting him? But again 1 thought of my mother's advice; "Beware of boys – the human devils roaming the world". What my mother omitted was the word 'lascivious' to limit the generalization, To me, every boy was thus a devil and this ideology was later to play very hard on me.

During the rest of the year this boy tried two or-three times to renew his application but finding that I never even returned his greetings, kept his distance and flirted about with other girls, some of whom were my mates and who readily accepted him. Even though he did everything to provoke me into being jealous, I did not by any means regret but I remained alone and satisfied.

Chapter 3

I continued dismissing one boy after another for I saw nothing good in them. By the time I reached Form IV, I was a complete mature woman at an age of 20 though a complete social misfit. Most of my mates flirted about with partners from CCAST Bambili which was considered a university in those days; from Sacred Heart College, and from Cameroon Protestant College, Bali. The influx of letters from these partners even though very clandestine, was very regular. Beautiful white and black pictures were always the contents of such letters, sometimes postcards with pictures of half-naked covers with a phase or two of love expressions.

Back from holidays especially, topics of conversation focused on boyfriends, romance, dancing and dating in general. The merits and demerits of each boy were discussed. Occasionally, I felt lost as I came out with no such story even though I tried making it up with boring stories of Christian Youth Fellowship cometogethers which sounded absurd to non-protestants. I was nicknamed the Virgin Mary a name I loathed terribly, but a name which nevertheless fitted so well,

Whenever it was drawing near to occasional days, every letter to my classmate proposed a rendezvous after the march past which usually took place at the Mankon Stadium. After marching the couples met at an appointed place, took some snap shots, did a bit of strolling and ended the day with tea-time dances either at the New City, Club 100 or People's Palace Night Club. During such days 1 always returned to school immediately after march-past because I would not have any mate with me whose program would not be a bore to my life. Sometimes, I persevered and stayed but the Sacred

Heart Boys would not give me a breathing space as they would always brake me and express their infinite degree of love, boys who had never even met me before and who seeing me for the very first time were capable of mounting dead love. Such incidents always forced me give up the day and return early.

Sometimes, of course, I regretted having returned too early to school especially when I found the school deserted and boring until the return of my mates after having reluctantly parted with their lovers. These friends would talk about the adventures of the day for the next two weeks.

I was without doubt one of the most beautiful girl in school but the most naive. Certain jealous girls thought that I had no time with boys because I had not seen anyone handsome enough to take my hand. I was accused of pride and segregation. This was of course a false deduction for I did not even know what criteria a girl used to choose her boy nor of what importance was the handsomeness of a devil.

Some of the boys who tried unsuccessfully to brake me on the way tried it by writing but I would not reply to such a letter and would tear it and burn.

It does not mean that I was completely devoid of human natural weaknesses. Some of the stories my friends made about their boys were somewhat of interest to me. I was secretly jealous of such stories and they often had an amorous provocation. I was internally disturbed. Sometimes I very much felt like seeing a boy and if possible touching him. One day, I dreamt during siesta that I was hugging my biology tutor who was the only male I saw every day in a school where boys were strictly forbidden. The next day when I met him in class, I very much felt like touching him.

During the cold nights of the dry season while in my bed

I was seized by strange imaginations. I suffered in this way for six months when an incident occurred to me, an incident which gives this narration its theme.

During one 20th May Day which Cameroonians consider the most important in the year (since it marks the Reunification between the two parts of the country) I was accompanied by my mate Collette who was a girl far more experienced than myself. She had a boyfriend in CPC (Cameroon Protestant College), Bali. This boy had made a rendezvous with her through writing and they were to meet at a particular place in the stadium after march-past. Collette had invited, me to accompany her to the spot but had not revealed to me that we were going to meet a boy. Knowing what programs after march-past always consisted of, I no doubt suspected everything but reluctantly followed her. We had some difficulty in sorting out this boy; out of the thick feast day crowd. When we finally met him, he was accompanied by another boy almost of the same build-up as he. He was a little bit darker than I and grew an afro. He had small squinted eyes with the superior lip thicker than the inferior which were black at the outward part, and charmingly red nearer inside.

We changed warm greetings and conversed cordially about the colorful occasion. I was very casual throughout the conversation and wished it would end quietly so that we could take our leave. But the conversation went on interminably .even though not involving a particular subject of importance. Also, throughout the conversation, I noticed that Collette's boy's companion was focusing his eyes straight into my face and all his questions were directed to me even if I showed little interest on the subject. Collette must have enjoyed the trend of affairs much as she was constantly

13

reminding me that the question was meant for me. I always gave very brief and evasive answers which this boy naughtily continued asking me to substantiate.

I was always seizing an opportunity of no more questions coming to ask for our leave when Collette's boy asked us to accompany them for a snapshot. I quickly shook my head scared by the fact that I will move with these boys side by side through the Commercial Avenue to the photography studio. I refused vehemently but Collette convinced me hard that her boy will pay the taxi for all four of us. I reluctantly gave in and we took a cab which dropped us at the Ever Ready Photos where we had some snapshots.

I breathed cold air after the photographer had fumbled with his instruments and flashed the extra strong rays into our eyes. I was already thinking that we had freed ourselves from these devils and that we would move back to school when a new danger arose.

The boys did not only propose that we go to the 1p.m. film but that we should go to a tea-time dance after. This was already too much and I could not help it any longer. I gave just no room for manners and gave the proposal an outright objection, asked Collette to escort me back to school and if she was not prepared, I would not worry taking my leave. She tried to convince me but to no avail. In addition, the new boy was already exceeding his bounds as he put his hands over my shoulder to slide a few tender words into my ear. I flung away his band from my shoulder so violently that my companions only had to reserve their comments. I was terribly annoyed, bid them goodbye and immediately turned and climbed the steps into the road and was moving away when someone called me from behind. When I turned I saw Collette panting behind me. She asked me not to disgrace her by exposing my primitiveness and that the whole group was coming to see me off.

The word 'primitiveness' checked my behavior and I seemed to realize what I had done. The group came up and as we were moving off, Collette's man asked me what I meant by all this behavior; if I was indirectly telling them that they were all criminals or sinners because they went to films and dances and if at all they were, was 99% of the western world's population sinners? Were they then condemned to embrace the eternal punishment while I alone would be saved?

The question sounded intelligent but I just ignored him and we moved on silently. Collette moved behind with her lover while this boy whose name I later knew to be Lesley, was struggling to keep up with a rhythm of majestical steps with me.

Chapter 4

There are moments when a woman wishes to liberate herself from her femininity and moments when she wishes to be much more feminine than actual. You never know how beautiful you are until you are confronted by a devout lover. The way nature has distributed beauty to human beings is very haphazard.

The human being has no influence on his beauty. He is subject to his beauty but his mouth is master of the beauty of others. One thing is certain; there are beautiful ones and ugly ones. In the love scene, there is no ugliness; both the beauty and the ugly become one thing; "the most beautiful I have seen in the world".

A man who is in love reserves no manly aspects. In front of his lover, he reduces himself to the state of an underdog. He accepts every condition his woman gives him on condition that she will spare him a bit of her love. A man who is asking for a woman's love and at the same time trying to show the woman that he still withholds his prestige and that her love is not too vital to his life, is not really in love. She is his oxygen and without this oxygen, he would die. A man in love is every day trying to gather all the fragments of prestige which would be of admiration of his loved one but every time he meets her, he unconsciously dispenses with this prestige and asks for sympathy. Prestige and sympathy are on opposite ends. All true love springs from sympathy rather than from prestige. A lover is thus a sympathizer.

Love is instinctive. No one can advise another one to love. You can never decide whether to be in love or not. The brain plays no part in love. Love is rather emotional. You are never aware of it until you find yourself already deep in it. Reasonableness gives way to instinct and instinct and stupidity are one. What you say is not the most reasonable nor the most logical but pell-mell.

The lover rambles nonsense and it is then left to the beloved to give in or give up not as a result of what has been learnt from this rambling but as a result of his or her own instinct.

To come back to my tale, Lesley who shall remain a nightmare to me until the end of my days put me in a situation in which rejection was equally as painful as acceptance, and death more welcoming.

We left Lesley when he was trying to keep a rhythm of majestical steps with me. I had suspected right from the first moment I met this boy that he and Collette had made a plan for me and was thus prepared for the battle. Everything he had to tell me had thus been suspected and would not be different from what scores of boys had told me. He would harp on the same string. He would sing the same tune on the same note. I was prepared to dismiss his questions with the briefest answers I could if at all I felt like answering him.

He started by asking me about my feelings for the great feast day.

'Fine'

'What are you going to do in school now?'

'Nothing'

'Are you going to read?'

'No'

'To do what then?'

'It concerns me alone!'

On and on came the questions. When shall the 'goodbyes' and the 'see you again' come? Then came the introduction which I did not need.

Lesley was struggling to keep up with a rhythm of majestical steps with mine

'Well Miss, my name is Lesley Njapa'. I was about to say 'so what?' but it stuck in my throat. 'And you Miss?' It was getting unbecoming. In fact, this boy was too daring. I had a good mind not to answer him but a good idea sprang into my mind that I should give him a wrong name to stop him from molesting my life.. I opened my lips to pronounce the wrong name.

'Evelyn' O Lord, what had I done? I had given the right name and what had I planned to do? I was already thinking of adding a false second name to falsify the whole name when

19

this boy surprised me not only by completing my true family name but by pronouncing even my third name with some dexterity.

'Evelyn Bih Ndangeh. Am I right?' I shuddered under the dexterity of this pronunciation of my own name by someone I had never seen nor learnt of before. Wonderfully astonished, I only emitted a guttural interjection.

'So you had known all? Why did you need to ask me again?' He cleared a cough and spoke again.

'Miss Evelyn Ndangeh. I have come to Mankon today purposefully to see you.'

'What?' I trembled at what he was saying. I could not help cutting in and looked at this bold fellow directly into his eyes for the very first time since I met him. 'Have you ever known me before? By the way, who are you and what is your problem with me?' I had spoken loudly, and Collette and her boy who were deep in a love conversation behind us must have heard as they instantly stopped their conversation and were listening to what I was saying. The boy too was silent for a moment during which I could hear some sweet music drifting from the Vicky Night Club into our ears. Two heavy damsels from the Providence Commercial College lumbered past us and nearly pushed us down amidst the thick 20th May crowd heading towards the direction of the music. Some others were moving and tapping their fingers at the rhythm of this music which as it came louder, r could clearly distinguish the voice of a singer struggling to mimic the celebrated Tim & Fotys 'Abesamo'. I was doing everything to forget that there was a perturber moving besides me when Lesley repeated his statement and this time he was even bolder and more emphatic.

'I have come to Mankon today purposefully to see you',

he said.

'Had you ever known me before?'

'Of course, too well'.

My brains ran fast and I tried to think of all the boys who had tried me at one time or another and had been rebuffed but I could not remember having met such a fellow.

'I spend all my midterms and some weekends in this town and 1 attend Sunday services at the Ntamulung Presbyterian Church where I always meet you.'

This could be true because I, being a Presbyterian by denomination used to attend Church services at Ntamulung, an exceptional, privilege given to Presbyterians in Our Lady of Lourdes which is Roman Catholic.

'What is your problem with me then?' I asked this question just for formality for 1 knew his problem well enough.

'Please Evelyn, I have a problem which if solved shall change both your life and mine'.

'Am I God?'

'Of course not, the first day I saw you, I developed a particular admiration for you and since then I have been haunted by your love. I have come to realize that without you by my side, my life would be worth nothing. Every night I dream of you. Every day I have visions about you. Even on the road I daydream about you. I have suffered immensely for want of your love. Last week, I told Willy, Collette's boy that there was no reason why I suffered in silence and that I would like to meet you and pour my heart to you. The meeting of today is not by coincidence but well-planned since two weeks. It is a well-organized rendezvous. Please Evelyn, love me. Take my hand. Be my own.'

Well spoken, I thought. I had prepared my answer to all

this babbling. A later answer was to be directed not only to Lesley but to the rest of the team which had planned the rendezvous without my knowledge. I was terribly annoyed, particularly at the idea that Collette could treat me as a fool, that she could carry me to sell to people as though I was a goat. No, this was enough.

'Well Mr. Lesley thanks very much for all the pains you have taken to come up to Mankon just to talk to me. Thanks too for loving me. Thank Willy and Collette for organizing this rendezvous without my knowledge. Just as you have worked yourself to love me, work yourself too to forget me and your illness shall be cured. If not, try another girl for there are millions in the world, most of them better than myself and more prepared to take you. So, Mr. Lesley, let me go.' I made a sudden change of direction and was almost skipping through the Commercial Avenue when he called on me very appealingly.

'A moment Evelyn, before coming to you, I knew that there were many girls in this world and even more beautiful ones as you say but I still chose you. It is not that I am unable to get any other girl. It is rather that I have a particular lust for your love and if you will deny me this love, I shall not get after any other girl and shall remain haunted by this repulsion until the end of my days. Dear, I know I have taken you too abruptly and would propose that you meditate over it and do not kill me with a rebuff.

Rubbish altogether, I thought. I could not help being impolite this time or this devil would not go away from me.

'Mr. Lesley please, I have said that you should forget about me. Go home and conceive no morbid imaginations. Liberate yourself of hallucinations before it is too late. Good luck in your search for a lover!'

He was still clearing his throat to continue his persuasion when I put an end to this insipid conversation with a very blunt declaration.

'Moreover man, I don't love anyone and if at all I were to love a boy, he would not be of your type' .

This was just a recitation I had learned from my friends. I did not even know what type of boy to love for I had never thought that I would one day love. Nevertheless, the bullet struck. Assailed by this declaration, he fell back to join Collette and Willy. I seized this opportunity to triple my steps and without any excuse, I disappeared.

After I had kept them a good distance away a wave of guilt seized me. What had I done? Had I not blundered? I shuddered. Across the street, numerous pairs were pacing up and down the street either going to the cinema or to tea time dances. Some of them who were my classmates contemptuously winked at me. I was doubting if I had behaved well towards this fellow. Again, what had this boy done to me? What did he want actually?

I have a particular lust for your love

Many questions rang in my head simultaneously and coupled up with some guilt, I almost made a roundabout turn to go back to the group in order to apologize for my bad behavior. I stopped moving and pondered a little.

A trickle of sweat ran over my face and dropped on my blouse. I took out a handkerchief and wiped it off. I looked back but the crowd on the street could not permit me distinguish who was who for it was too thick. Moreover if I went back what would I say? To withdraw the statement I had made to him would mean I loved him. Just a mere apology of my poor behavior would be interpreted as love. No. It was better to leave it as it was. I had behaved rightly. I then moved back to school but on the way I was still feeling bad and guilty. I tried to forget and to think of something else but the picture of this boy called Lesley was still roaming in my mind. I tried to sleep but no, Lesley. I took my books, went to the class and pretended to read but no, Lesley. I stood up, shook off myself thought of something else and came back to read but discovered that I was reading the same sentence over and over. I myself started conceiving the strange imaginations I had forbade Lesley. I was imagining what he was doing in town at that moment I was struggling to read. I almost felt like crying when I remembered him having said he had come up to Mankon purposefully to see me. I had left him in the lurch in town.

When Collette finally returned, I felt terribly guilty to meet her and was not able to look at her in the face. I had planned to reproach her seriously but soon found that I could not. I thought she would make an allusion to the incident it: town, so that I could vindicate myself or even apologize but to my greatest disappointment she remained very silent and reserved. What a chagrin. She avoided m} company for the rest of the time and I only eavesdropped her one day complaining to another classmate of ours that I had disappointed her during the feast day with a very unbecoming attitude in front of her friends.

For the rest of the academic year I was a patient. No one knew my illness nor could it be diagnosed by any doctor. Always Lesley, the boy who must have trained himself to forget me. I was burning with a desire to see this boy again.

My secret illness was aggravated by the arrival of the pictures we had taken on the 20th May feast day. Collette gave my own card without a comment. The cards were beautiful. I stood between Collette and Lesley and William stood next to Collette, two real couples. I didn't know where to keep this card. I was ashamed to expose it and I could neither hide it because I wanted to be looking at it at every moment. This was rather an embarrassment to me. At one time, I put it under my pillow but when making up my bed, it always fell to the ground and inquisitive eyes protruded. Under my box, it took me too much time to rummage books and dresses to make a glimpse of it again.

I wanted to see Lesley in person and talk to him. He had of course, given me time to meditate and answer him afterwards but he had not precised when he would meet me again. It was the last school term and no occasion was coming up again in which we could meet. Moreover, he was doing his last year in the secondary school and would be very much engaged with the GCE and thus might never come up to town again. I nevertheless hoped against hope that he would come and that the next time I met him I would tell him that he was free to love me. I could not deduce what all this would mean but no matter the consequences, I would speak.

The next Sunday, I went to Ntamulung Presbyterian Church wishing very much to see him there. After the Church service, I lingered around the Church premises in search of him but was not blessed with his presence. I tried again the next two weekends but luck could not smile on me.

My relations with Collette again became cordial but she made sure she dealt with me with a long spoon when it concerned the social field. I too had not the head to speak out my emotions to her. About the pictures, I only told her that they were very beautiful. Whether she deduced anything from this statement, she did not tell me.

I thus suffered in this way up to the end of the academic year without ever seeing Lesley or having any news about him. My 4th year in school ended, my maidenhood still untarnished with.

After the church services, I lingered around the church premises.

Chapter 5

Spending my summer holidays in the village, I lost all hopes of ever meeting Lesley but did not by any means forget him. His picture was always hidden for if my mother or father saw it, I would be in chains. At times I would lock up my small room which I shared with my two younger brothers, take the card and have a satisfactory study of it and keep it back.

One bright morning, towards the end of the holidays, I sat with my elder cousin's radio outside our house while trying to grasp over a novel when the broadcaster instantly cut a record I very much appreciated and started an announcement. I was exasperated for this was a record that had very much appealed to me Jim Reeves' *'Precious Lord lead me home'*. I was just about to tum off the radio when the broadcaster precised that the announcement was very important to candidates who had applied to enter the Cameroon College of Arts, Science and Technology, Bambili. My attention was captured and I raised the volume of the radio for many Class V students in my school who had passed the GCE were already waiting for the common entrance results to enter the high schools. I very much wanted to know which of them were admitted. The candidates were listed in order of merit. I listened very attentively arid wished the first candidate would be a student from Lourdes for they had scored a very high percentage at the GCE. I shuddered at the mention of the first name.

'Njapa Lesley...' I did not hear the rest of the names. Presently my sufferings started. 'Suffering' might not really be the right word but it describes the degree of my worry. I was

28

divided between happiness and sadness, happy at his success and sad for not being able to own him all for myself.

In those-days,' CCAST Bambili was the highest institution in the Anglophone provinces of Cameroon. It was a prestige having a boy in this institution. During feast days, they would march in suits and ties while the other schools wore mean uniform. It was not of course the prestige having a hoy in CCAST that concerned me but the fact that he would hence fourth spend the public feast days in Mankon as it was obligatory for students from CCAST Bambili and I would thus have the opportunity to meet him. I decided and swore that when next I met him, I would tell him that I was mad in love with him and that he should take me into his hands before I died.

The holidays came to an end. We went back to school and my friends started boring me with their interminable stories of boyfriends, dating, dancing and all what not. I did not hate them this time but was jealous. The school regulations this time were revised and made more stringent. Our principal who was making her second year in the administration began putting her policies into practice. All mid-terms and outings which permitted us go out of the school borders were abolished. Even visiting days were abolished, that is days which relations were permitted to visit us in school. All letters to students of Our Lady of Lourdes were henceforth to be indiscriminately opened and read and any deemed immoral or implicating was to be posted to the students' parents or sponsor. They would be summoned and the student warned in front of them if at all she escaped suspension. The list of relatives who were permitted to write to each student was cut from ten to five and this was limited to father, mother, sisters and brothers and any letter from a cousin or from an uncle would be put in the list of palaver letters. Henceforth, any girl caught moving or standing with a boy aimlessly anywhere in town, no matter the period of the year (holidays included) would be automatically dismissed from school.

All the above mentioned regulations had little or nothing to do with me for throughout my four years, I had never had any occasion to go either on midterm or outing, receive visitors in school or talk with boys in town. I had of course received some implicating letters but the senders seemed to have known that it was hard in our school and always sent them very clandestinely and not receiving any replies ceased. I would not have therefore been very affected if the regulations had ended here. But two more were added which gave me a serious blow. Presbyterian students were until further notice to organize their Sunday services in a classroom in the school rather than going to Presbyterian Churches in town. Secondly, after march-past during official feast days, students were to proceed immediately back to school and roll call would be made one hour after the march-past.

Even this would have meant nothing to me in my earlier days in school and I would have praised my principal for this step in her administration. Unfortunately, I was no more the insensitive Evelyn I used to be. Natural weaknesses were already playing a part in me. I had come back to the 5th year, determined to make a man hunt. This as occasion permitted, would have been made either at the Presbyterian Church in Ntamulung or during official feast days in town after the march-past. Moreover if I were by chance to meet this man in town, I would be faced with a devil's alternative; try to catch him and face the risk of being thrown out of school or lose him and bear all the consequences of this loss while safeguarding my place in school. To expect that this man shall one day come to Bafut for holidays or that I would meet him somewhere else out of Mankon town was a dream. I weighed all these possibilities and came to a conclusion that all doors were closed ahead of me and that it was better to forget altogether of ever meeting Lesley.

Even though my friends were not more hard hit than myself, they complained bitterly that their lives in school and in the whole division had been reduced to that of prisoners. They argued that Our Lady of Lourdes was only a girls college, not a women's prison. They could only grumble and no one could dare talk to the hearing of any of the Sisters who governed us.

For the whole of the first term until we went for holidays no official occasion took us to town. The second term which was supposed to be a very serious one for class V students who were preparing for their mock and GCE exams started very badly for me. Academic work became very tedious for we were to finish our syllabuses and revise before entering for the numerous end of course examinations which awaited us. Unfortunately for me I was attacked by a serious and mysterious bellyache which embarrassed every doctor in the Mankon General Hospital. Everything I ate was vomited despite all sorts of anti-vomiting medicine I took.

I lay in the hospital for a week and the doctors, not being able to stop the vomiting nor even able to diagnose the illness asked my parents to take me to a native doctor. I was therefore transferred to a herbal home at Oku As is ever the case with almost all native doctors, I was diagnosed and believed to have been poisoned by a boy who wanted to marry me and I refused. Luckily my family was a staunch Christian family and we covered our ears to all such beliefs and only appealed to him to do his best to cure me. After two weeks of fumbling with herbs, exorcism and very seldom sleep, I felt better and strong enough to au back to school.

I have not yet been convinced up to date that I was cured by this herbalist for he did not seem to be sure of each remedy he gave me and everything was rather by trial and error. He would rub certain ointments in my face and would tell me that I would dream about certain persons and particular incidents but I never saw nor thing nor did I even sleep. At times he would give me some herbs to eat and would tell me to expect particular effects but it still failed. Worst of all, he told wonderful lies at divining some which would have caused serious problems between me and my parents if not, thanks to God, my parents did not believe in divining. He told my parents that the author of my illness was a former fiancé whom I had refused after having incurred much spending from this boy. This boy was thus keeping a piece of my dress and my hair.

He said the illness would still return if something serious was not done. He charged my parents terrible sums and goats to block me from the boy's powers and when my parents confessed that they were not able to pay such an amount because they were not rich enough, he proposed to my parents to give me to him for a wife so that he could cure me free of charge.

My parents asked him to give them time so that I could go and finish my school while they consulted relations. Back at home, my parents interviewed me seriously and since I had never failed them or given them any room to suspect, they damned consequences and we organized a thanksgiving ceremony in Church on my behalf, prayed and I returned to school. I still do believe that without going to the hospital, I would have still been cured by the will of God. All the same the herbal home gave me an experience, as I was later to jot down the name of the native doctor as one of my_suitors, even though only second to Lesley. Time and again, I was tempted to believe what the native doctor had said and suspected Lesley for being the cause of my illness. This would be very unrealistic for, one; my relationship with Lesley had never gone farther than a handshake and an exchange of a few words. Where could he then get a piece of my dress, not even to mention my hair of my body? Two, Lesley was still young and as innocent in herbs as myself and moreover, a good Christian of the Presbyterian Church. How could Lesley do this? No, I could not believe. I loved Lesley and would have him.

I was completely convalescent after having missed four good weeks of school and prepared to return to school. My father called me and gave me certain necessary pieces of advice.

'My daughter' he had said, 'You know that you are the only eye in our family. You know the family is looking on you for its future prosperity. You have also realized how your mother and I are struggling just to buy your school equipment. Luckily for us, the government has saved us from the burden of school fees by giving you a scholarship or else, you would not have been a student today. Take care of deviations. Concentrate on your book. Do not compare or even mix with the children of the rich. There is always an opening for them in case of failure. They would be sent to study overseas or they would have big jobs in the capital. If you fail, no one will take care of you. This could be the end of your studies and you would not even have a responsible man who would assure you of your future. Worst of all, your younger brothers and sisters who are looking up to you for their future would become useless".

'Beware of boys' interrupted my mother who had long been expecting my father to touch this topic but had been disappointed. 'Whether' the native doctor was telling the truth or lying we are not yet able to prove"

'No Mama, it was a big lie', I cried out not being able to bear this accusation any longer. 'I have never had a boyfriend, not even to talk of a betrothed.'

'I am not of course believing in what the doctor said', my mother corrected; 'I only want to let you know one truth. You are already a big girl, in fact, ripe for boys. They will run after you now and promise you all sorts of things, the rich ones would promise sponsoring your junior ones, when you are full, they would abandon you. Keep them out of your way. You are a man in your own family and when you shall have a good stand in future, God shall give your own partner'.

'Thank you mama, I shall not fail you', I said but inwardly guilty of my secret plans for Lesley. This had been the most solemn moment I had had with my parents. My two younger brothers were all in classes six and seven in the primary school and were a great burden to my parents who had no regular income. They paid their fees by selling foodstuffs in the market, ranging from 'garri' produced by my mother, cocoyams, yams, plantains and when it became hard they sold brooms. With what they earned from this, they spent almost all on three of us and there was hardly anything left to cloth their own selves, My four most junior sisters and brothers had just no dream of ever going to school.

I took the taxi at the Bafut Three Corners to go back to school. On the way, I contemplated seriously at the advice my parents had given me the previous evening I thought of my junior ones who were still illiterate and counting on me for their future. I thought of Lesley's earnest appeal to be his partner and promise that if I accepted, it would change our lives till the end of our days. This just coincided with what my mother said; boys would give very sweet promises just to satisfy their lusts after which, they, would disappear. Was this really what Lesley wanted? Moreover, what was so particular in Lesley that made me love him so much? Could not I have another Lesley in future after I must have had a good stand to sponsor my brothers? It was really reasonable enough to forget of all boys, Lesley included, and struggle for our future.

The taxi came to a halt at the Bamenda motor park. I had been lost in contemplation and had not realized the distance even though the vehicle was wonderfully uncomfortable for it was a Renault 4 meant for four passengers but which carried seven of us. I had shared the back seat with four passengers and the driver had shared his cabin with two.

I took my small hand bag in which were my three dresses and toilet material and started moving to school on foot for I had not much money to spare some for a cab. I thought of my friends back at school who would be very glad to see me: Collette, Gladys, Mariana etc. I imagined how much work I would still have left for the exams since I had absented myself for a whole month.

I tried to walk fast but still weak from my illness and the month being February, it was hot and dry. At the Commercial Avenue, vehicles moved very slowly for the road was terribly bumpy as a result of potholes which had not been refilled for the past four years. In front of the Bamenda Market main gate, there was a traffic jam and vehicles were slower than pedestrians. .

When I had just bypassed this main gate, the inscription on a Volkswagen bus which had been trapped in the middle of some vehicles and which was struggling to free itself, attracted my attention. In black, the inscription read 'CCAST Bambili' The vehicle was full with students and I did not immediately think of who I could know inside. Just for curiosity sake, I flashed a glance at the occupants and finding that all were boys, I turned away my glance, overtook the vehicle struggling to free itself and moved on.

About a hundred meters further up, the traffic was loose and I could move freely on the tarmac when a vehicle started hooting behind me. I stepped off the tarmac to the side of the road and turned to find out that the hooting vehicle was the CCAST Volkswagen I had bypassed. I was arrested by a sudden heartbreak when a head protruded out of the front seat on my own side and fixed a look on me.

This was the particular figure I had been looking for almost a year. It looked more handsome and appealing than ever. The look was naive and serene. At that particular moment, I completely forgot of the advice my parents had given me the previous evening arid would be prepared to follow Lesley if at that moment he said 'Come and let's go'.

I waved but he did not return it nor did he even behave as if he had ever seen me before. I stood there aghast and would have run after the bus if it had stopped but it ran faster and faster disappearing behind vehicles. I at every moment wished it to come to a halt but I was disappointed.

I was very confused with Lesley's behavior. I did not know if he had recognized or he had merely ignored me. If the former; why had he given me a particular look and even told the driver to hoot at me? No matter what he thought, I comforted myself that he had not recognized me and had looked at me with no particular interest just as somebody he had known before but had forgotten where and when.

I would have exploded with excitement if 1 did not tell someone that I had seen him. Back in school, I told Collette but pretended to be indifferent.

'Where did you see him?'

'In their school bus, moving towards Big Mankon'.

'Did he see you?'

'I do not think for I waved and he did not return it. Even if he did, I do not think he might have recognized me'.

'He did recognize but refused to wave back', Collette mocked and went straight into my heart hut I forced myself to argue back.

"I am not convinced".

Collette just let loose a derisive smile and moved away not knowing how far she had infuriated me.

Chapter 6

I worked hard to cover up my school work I had lost. Each time I thought of my family and then Lesley, I was guilty and confused.

I was again blessed with another opportunity of meeting him before my last school year in the secondary school came to a close. This was again, a 20th May Day, the 1st Anniversary of our meeting with him. This time, it was no more on rendezvous but purely coincidental.

We had marched before the CCAST students and I took my place at the side of the marching track to watch the students of this institution pay their own respect to the national tricolor. It had always been complained that these students walked rather than marched past the flag. I had never taken any particular interest to look at them during such an occasion. This day, I was a life-witness to this contemptuous behavior of some of the elements of this institution who walked past the flag while conversing with their friends. Some pocketed their hands and some were busy exchanging cigarettes and lighters while still in front of the flag. This was really strange to me and I found the CCAST students very despicable except one person I was in search of.

I did not of course expect to see him march with the first two halls which were all girls' halls for they marched following the hostels in which they stayed in school. The first hall was the Peace Hall and the second the Unity Hall The next placard read 'Independence Hall' and all the boys wore blue suits. I scrutinized starting from the boy who carried the placard to the last boy. But I did not see Lesley.

I was beginning to be disappointed but soon a fourth

placard emerged and read 'Reunification Hall'. My eye moved from one line of students to the next. When the first half had passed I wished that he could be among the second half. To my greatest dismay, this half too was destitute of Lesley. What had happened? Was he ill'! Was he in CCAST Bambili at all? Was he even alive'? But I saw him in their school bus the other day.

Confused, I reluctantly moved away hut hoped that my scrutiny had not been thorough enough. Just then, I realized that we were expected in school an hour after march-past and that I had already wasted thirty minutes in a fruitless search. I still had thirty minutes to move to school. 1 looked around and found just none of our school mates. Even Collette who would have been my companion for the day and who would have been loitering around town with her boy had not taken the risk of moving any more with me. She too was nowhere to be found and might have already been reaching the school compound. I would be penalized if I did not regain the compound in the next few minutes.

Terribly afraid, I started rushing back to school. I forgot altogether about Lesley and tried to see how many steps I could take in a second in order to escape suspension from school. When I reached the Post Office junction, I saw the back of probably the last students branching off to take the short course through the Providence Commercial College compound. I started racing to catch up with them but soon found that I could not, for they were a good distance away and I was not a good spotter.

By the time I reached the PCC (Providence Commercial College) compound, I was panting and sweating. I saw some two figures moving towards me from the opposite direction. The taller and darker of the two broke an amicable smile and

I, not thinking of meeting anybody I could know focused my eyes on the ground. I put up my eyes again just when I was about to step on the tarmac road and was already abreast with this figure. I was already too close to him to prepare for this devilish meeting.

With sweat running down my face, my panting steadily increasing, I was terribly shocked to meet Lesley. This was the worst moment. My heartbeat went at a terrific speed. For the first few seconds, I was petrified. When I came back to myself, I did not know how to behave.

'A happy feast day Miss Evelyn' he greeted. He spoke with, much courtesy, not even as one I had ever maltreated. Trembling, I mumbled out my own greetings.

We were in the open street and could be detected from any angle, especially the school uniform I wore which was very conspicuous. Secondly, time was dead against me. A few more minutes and the roll call would be finished. A few minutes after, the principal would be driving around the town searching for her culprits. If she were to meet me just a few hundreds of meters from the school, talking with a boy, it would be the end of me in school. There was Lesley standing in front of me, fresh and as handsome as ever in his blue suit, a white shirt inside the vest and a multicolored tie. This was Lesley himself, not his picture. Would I again lose him this time? The cards were there in front of me and I needed to choose the black one. I would be landed nose first into the abyss if I chose wrongly. The moment was very poorly chosen for this game. I left all to destiny.

His companion who was all the time looking into my eyes while I was struggling to wipe the sweat from my face was no more Willy, Collete's boy but someone else I had never seen before.

I answered all the questions without the least thought, faltering throughout the conversation.

'Are you moving back to school as usual?'

This was Lesley himself, not his picture.

'Yes', I little realized that this question was sarcastic

The more he stood there, the more I shivered and gave an impromptu answer without having understood the question.

His friend seemed to have realized that I was nervous and put his hand into his trouser pocket and brought out some chewing gum which he shared to us starting from me.

'Would you mind having one, Miss?'

'No, yes, no, not at all, thanks! I faltered and took one. This was no remedy for my nervousness.

'Long time, not seen you' Lesley continued

'Long really'

'I am now in CCAST Bambili'

'I did not know' I'd lied.

'It is hot, isn't it?' His friend asked me.

'Very'

'Would you mind accompanying us to the next off license where we can have a cool down and escape this blazing afternoon sun?'

Just what I had longed for. I almost turned and start making straight for the spot but quickly realized myself. Questions starting with 'would you mind' had ever been my problem. To give a positive answer to such a question you have to say 'No'. To answer negatively, you have to say' Yes'. This had been our problem in class even though I had taken time to learn it and had known which word to use when; Due to nervousness, I did not take time to ponder on which was which. Thinking that I was answering positively, I said 'Yes'

I had made this mistake before and had struggled to correct myself. This time I was ashamed to make another correction. All the same, the conversation was continuing and a solution would be reached. I was afraid that he could withdraw this proposal. I would die. Another unwelcoming question followed.'

'Are you much in a hurry?' I quickly cleared my throat to say 'no' and even to add that I had something to tell him and that we actually needed a place to sit and talk

The mouth is the greatest traitor of the human body. Not all what is intended in the mind is said by the mouth. The converse of this statement is not all what is said by the mouth is intended by the mind. While actually turning to move to the spot, I heard my mouth say;

'Very much in a hurry', Lord, I had again blundered, I realized what I had said only when the sentence had been articulately produced. I was thinking that he would press hard his invitation so that I could withdraw my statement but I was disappointed. He simply said.

'I see, hope next time will do'.

The invitation was therefore dropped. Lesley might have taken it to be very normal of my character. He did not seem to be disappointed or in any way surprised at this refusal while I was burning with an ambition to sit with Lesley and converse. How could I withdraw that dirty statement without involving myself in ignominy? Where could I take the head to do this?

Still lost in this confusion, Lesley's aching 'goodbye' reached my ears. I hesitated, for some time before giving the inevitable answer to this farewell. Lesley's friend, a very sensitive boy seemed to have noticed my hesitancy and looked straight and questioningly into my eyes, then to Lesley. Confused and ashamed, I started moving away very sluggishly, at every moment expecting him to call back but he and his friend moved unconcernedly towards the off license bar and disappeared inside it.

As I moved through the St. Joseph's primary School compound my mind was away. Only my body was lumbering up the hill and something was constantly telling me to go back and meet them in the off-licence bar. I of course knew what was awaiting me in the compound for I was already ten minutes late and how could I tell that I had not been seen standing with Lesley.

I was already a dead goat and needed not fear any knife. I was trying to shoot two birds with one stone. 'Go back to Lesley your man. Pour out your heart to him'. Another secret voice was admonishing me of how much debasement of myself this would be. It was not even the place of a girl to run after a boy. I thought of going back with the pretension of buying something from this off license bar but only drinks were sold in off license bars and I had refused to go and drink, what else would they expect me to buy there? Judging from Lesley's character, he would not even be prepared to open up any conversation since I had given him the impression that I was in a hurry.

I had no other alternative than to go back to school and face the devil. I groped my way up the hill as a donkey. It was only a few weeks to the summer holidays and this was my last year in this institution, maybe, as a student. All hopes of ever seeing Lesley again were dead slim since no other occasional days were forthcoming. I was ever locked up in the village for holidays. Where could I see Lesley again?

Except I went to CCAST Bambili High School; but was I sure of passing my examination? Was even I sure of continuing in Our Lady of Lourdes secondary school after that day? With all these heavy thoughts in my mind, I sat down by the side of the road and wept bitterly and only a hooting vehicle chased me from this spot.

Here again was to begin many weeks of internal suffering.

As I moved through the St. Joseph's school Mankon only my body was lumbering up the hill to Lourdes.

I reached school, fifteen minutes late for the roll call and fortunately for me, no sister was around. Only the school senior prefect caught me and not having known me to be heady or ever caught committing offences kept it secret. She knew what awaited me if she was to take me up to the principal. She interviewed me but terribly guilty, I could not even answer any question of hers.

'Evelyn, I am speaking to you, where did you go to?' She pretended to be serious. 'If you cannot speak I shall make you speak by taking you up to the Principal' I knew she could not do it being my, classmate and both of us facing the GCE which was to begin in less than a fortnight's time.

Not only our Senior Prefect was surprised. Collette especially who knew me so well and who knew that I knew no one in town, was the most dismayed.

'Evelyn, what happened? Were you ill? What? Please tell me'.

But no, I could not tell the truth about Lesley, not to Collette.

'Nothing', I answered.

'No, Evelyn, there is something, did you meet Lesley, any other boy?' I shook my head but, at least, the guilt on my face could convince Collette that I was with a boy.

'No one, I just felt like lingering in town a bit before returning'.

Collette was convinced that I was lying. I had never lingered in town before since five years of my stay. As usual she reserved her comments and went away.

Nothing else very particular occurred until the end of the term. June came. We wrote the final examination after which I bid my final adieu to my alma mater and went home for holidays. I was then quite a big girl and even in social circles, I was regarded with some respect. In my days, it was rare to see a girl go through the secondary school without setbacks ranging from lack of school fees, dismissal as a result of poor academic work, forced marriage to even pregnancy. One deserved congratulations not only for having passed the GCE but for having broken through these obstacles.

A secondary school leaver could teach in the primary school, in the other secondary commercial colleges and even in his own former college: I was thus a very respectable woman in my village especially in social circles and soon had some friction with my parents,

During this summer holidays, I was invited to serve as a hostess or as a receptionist in ballroom dances and since we were few, a secondary school graduate as I was, could not escape the notice of organizers. The importance of my august presence in dances could not be underestimated. I was sure to get class A invitation cards for every party, be it public or private.

At first my parents could not permit me attend such occasions. They still regarded me as, a child who needed protection and always held me back when the organizers came to take me out. The educated and more responsible persons of the village soon found it too unbecoming and intervened.

It was when I was invited to serve as a receptionist during a village community fund raising dance. The Divisional officer himself was to be present including numerous very important personalities. The chief organizer who was a primary school headmaster had come to our compound three days before to take me along to attend the organization committee meeting but my father told him that I could not go out.

'Look Papa', the headmaster had said, 'a child belongs to the parents alone when it is still in the womb. After birth the child is no more for the parents alone but for the government. Know that Evelyn is a government child now and needs to be used by it',

'Dear headmaster' my father had replied, 'You people have learnt book but also know that we have studied the tradition What do you mean by government? The government has its police, its messengers, its civil servants and so forth; it pays these persons for their services. Why can't they take them to come and serve during this occasion?'

'If my daughter is destroyed, shall the government ever come to care for her in this compound? By the way, we are not government workers and have never got a franc of the government, The government only knows us when it comes to work?' This had been my mother's argument who had all the while hated the headmaster.

'No mama you lie and you papa, you don't really know who is the government'. The headmaster had continued. 'The government is not only the president, his ministers and the divisional officers.' Even you papa, you're the government. I am the government. Everybody who is working for the well-being of the nation is a government man'.

The headmaster, being a good politician chose his words very well in order to convince my parents.

'The dance is a fund raising dance for the building of the bridge which links Njinteh with Niko. How do you know if tomorrow, Evelyn will not be wanting to build a story building in this compound. Where then shall the vehicle pass to come and throw stones here?"

When he saw that my father seemed convinced he turned to my mother. 'Mama, you say you have never eaten a franc of the government. Let me prove to you that you have. You did not help in digging the trunk A road which connects Bafut with Bamenda. Yet it takes you less than thirty minutes to go to Bamenda by car, a journey you would have taken not less than five hours to make by trekking. Next Evelyn has just completed from the secondary school. You forget that she was on government scholarship for all five years. Was this not government money?'

'You are right my son' my mother replied. 'My problem is only about protection. Who is responsible for the protection of my daughter during such night occasions? I ask this question because tomorrow when my daughter is pregnant, I would not see any of you here, even you, headmaster.'

The headmaster would have been embarrassed by this question but being a good orator, he muddled it out and left my parents spellbound.

'Evelyn is now a big woman, in fact a government woman. Very soon she will be sent to teach hundreds of kilometers away from you. She might even be sent to go and work with the minister himself in the big capital. More still, she might be sent flying like a bird to go and study overseas in the white man's land. Shall any of you be there to protect her?'

Excited by this good luck the headmaster was wishing on me, my parents laughed out and the headmaster felt proud to display his political ability to convince them.

'Don't you people know that the whole village is proud of Evelyn. If it were even possible, we would carry Evelyn around so that every girl can see her and copy her example. We even intend to introduce her to the Senior Divisional Officer himself as the most learned woman in the village. We shall make the Senior Divisional Officer appoint her as the leader of all the women of this part of the country'. Everyone laughed and cheered.

Since this day, my parents were permitting me to go out without much argument. As for me personally, I did not have much enthusiasm in attending parties but my learned position constrained me to respect these invitations. Many a time, I was called up to compose the sentences which were to appear on the invitation cards and even on the posters, I would also be given public speeches to edit and correct the language. I was thus indispensable.

Most or all of these occasions used to take place in the night. This was when I realized that I needed a boy for a partner. I attended parties alone and found myself out of place as the other girls were always paired. During dances especially, I was rough handled and there would be no one to protect me. Whenever anyone offered to protect me, he would later on want to become my predator.

Later on, I was inviting my cousin to accompany me to these dances but he soon became inconsistent and unpredictable in his comportment. After the dance, he would prefer escorting home his girl than me, thereby leaving me at the mercy of human tigers.

I thus made up my mind to try my hand at choosing a partner. During one students' meeting, I picked a boy, a man I would say, an ex-student of the Teacher's Training College, Batibo. He was kind, friendly and gentle. His weakness was that he was terribly dirty and old-fashioned in his way of dressing. He was always amongst the last persons to abandon a moribund fashion. He was very hard at resisting criticisms. He very much believed in individualism.

It was a great surprise when people saw me moving with him. I was seriously criticized by my friends for choosing a 'ballad' (as teachers were popularly called) as a friend. These criticisms had not of course, much to do with me. What prompted me to choose this man was his amicability but I was later on to find that even with this, I was not satisfied. Deep inside me I had just no love for him and dropped him after a month.

Still compelled by social repercussions to have a partner, I tried another fellow, a young, handsome gallant from the only government bilingual secondary and high school in the western state. He was a big contrast to the teacher for his tastes were not only modern but exaggeratedly artificial and utopian. He was the first boy in the village to wear the highest heeled shoes and the large leg trousers popularly known in those days as 'apaga' and 'salamander'. He smoked very fat and long cigars and it was even believed that he was an addict of marijuana. I could not say exactly if he loved me wholly. What I realized was rather that he was up to exploit my womanness. What he expected from me was neither my companionship nor my love. According to him, sexual relationship between a boy and his girl was the cause of love, not its result. He thus expected me to offer sexual satisfaction before he could love me wholly. This was very uncompromising with me and I knew that even if I satisfied him this way, the situation would not be different for he was a lover of too many girls, all of whom he promised marriage. I soon found that I could not cope with this fellow, not only because of his waywardness but because I myself couldn't love him even at his best moments. I parted with him just before the end of the holidays but still preserved my virginity.

I attended parties alone and the others were always paired

My cousin preferred escorting home his girl.

Chapter 7

Fortune did not desert me. The G.C.E. examination results were released and I learnt that I had passed in 7 subjects. Three weeks later, High School Common Entrance results were released and I was offered a place in CCAST Bambili.

At last, the dream had been realized. Everything had occurred so naturally and incidentally that I soon found myself registered in the arts class in Bambili.

The day I entered the 'campus' as it was called in those days, I was determined not to let any opportunity slip away. Even if he were not to approach me, I would approach him. If one had asked me why I loved Lesley so much, I wouldn't have been able to say why. I knew little or nothing about his tastes. I was convinced that he was the real man I wanted and it seemed that even if I were to discover that his character was worse than those of my former boys, it wouldn't matter much. I would fall in love with his vices.

For the first few days, Lesley was nowhere to be found in the campus. Where was Lesley? I learnt from a friend that some students had left the school prematurely to study abroad while others had withdrawn and were pursuing, professional courses in other institutions. My heart started beating. What would I do if Lesley was no more in CCAST Bambili? After a week, my fears were crowned when the list of second year students came out and Lesley's name was conspicuously absent. I still did not lose hope but weeks and almost months drifted away slowly and Lesley's absence became more and more evident. I swore that if Lesley were to be abroad, I would enter the convent and would only leave it if he came back to take my hand.

I struggled resiliently with my dilapidating hope but each new day looked duller than the former. I started an inquiry about his whereabouts from second year students who all proved to be in dark. The most a few knew about him was that he used to spend his holidays in Bafoussam and in Yaoundé but this information was too blurred.

Pairs sprang up in the compound at a speed of lightening. Most of the girls in the lower sixth paired with upper sixth boys and a few of them paired with their classmates. Many boys approached me but I couldn't risk it for Lesley could be somewhere still coming. I was however miserable when it came to parties which in CCAST Bambili were in a concatenation. Even some of my teachers came up to me to ask for friendship but little did know that my burning desire was to grab a body which was lost somewhere in the void.

Chapter 8

A few weeks to the end of the first term, I was attacked by an abscess on my left lap. I was referred to the Provincial Hospital in Bamenda. The school bus being down, I had to take a taxi.

When I stood at the Three Comers Bambili waiting for a cab, a white Peugeot swept past me and the driver slammed at his brakes a few meters ahead of me. There were too many passengers and the taxis were few. The passengers rushed to the Peugeot and each was struggling to have a seat.

Since I was limping, I arrived the car too late when it was already full and even overloaded. The driver was shouting and dragging out the overloaded passengers. My eyes were still wandering inside to search for a place in which I could squeeze myself just to reach the hospital.

'Evelyn' a voice pronounced my name from inside the car. I carried up my eyes to look at the person who had called me. Who did I see? Lesley. The real Lesley, not his shadow. He himself. A serious heartbreak flashed. For a few seconds I was not myself. Before I could return the greetings, the car was already moving.

'I am going to the hospital'. He said popping out his head through the window. 'We might meet in town'.

'Where?' The car had gone far and I couldn't hear what he said. Since I was also going to the hospital, I believed that I would meet him there.

Imagine how a child feels when he finds again his Christmas toy he thought lost forever. Imagine how a woman would feel if she were told that her husband who was believed to have been killed during the Second World War has come back. My readers can look for any metaphor which can qualify my feelings at the time. I will only say that my happiness was inexpressible.

I quickly imagined how our couple would look like back in school. I made a few useless comparisons. I was a daydreamer from there right to the hospital. Even though 1 sat on a very hard seat in the back of a Peugeot pickup, I did not feel any pains of the abscess which had kept me up all through the night again.

That day, the abscess was incised and I was hospitalized for 4 days just to prevent me from moving so that the wound could heal. A few students learnt of the hospitalization and came to my ward. Lesley had also learnt of it and accompanied them.

They chatted with me at random and each wished me a quick recovery and returned to school. I wished that Lesley could be the last to leave so that we could talk on past events and vindicate ourselves. He did not leave with the others but did not intend to leave last. He did not even intend, to stay with me. He invited the last girl who remained with me to move along with him. I was wonderfully jealous. This was again not a time for chances. This was the moment to strike.

Throughout the conversation with colleagues, I had not directed any personal question to Lesley. I had many things to learn about him, where he had been, whether he still had me in mind. I took a bold step, dismissed the other girl and told Lesley to stay.

'I have a private message for Lesley" I told the girl who sneered and took her leave.

'I hope the conversation shall be short for I myself, I am in a hurry'. Lesley said as though to make me nervous. I gathered myself and spoke boldly not betraying nervousness.

'I had almost thought you would not come back. Where have you been since the beginning of the year?' My boldness astonished him. He sat down on one of the hospital stools very near the bed and looked at me amazingly.

'I am surprised to hear you talk in this way, Miss Evelyn. Were you thinking about me?'

'Of course, I did and have ever done. Since I came to this school, I have ever thought of seeing you somewhere in the compound'.

'I was abroad with a brother. By the way, who told you that I was in CCAST Bambili?'

'I knew since the day the results were read over the radio'.

'How did you know that I went there? How could you tell that I hadn't made another choice?' He was following up one question with another. I thought of telling him that I had seen him in the CCAST bus one day in town but this would betray my pride. I would prove to him that I had been after him. But was it not necessary?

'A friend told me' It proved to him that I had monitored his progress but I did not care.

'You asked or how did the-friend come about talking to you about me?' Lord, what was Lesley up to again with this incessant questioning? All the same, I was prepared for everything.

'I asked'. I had shot wide. What would he think? This was me who two years back had been as proud as a cock, stooping low to this very Lesley who stooped low to me. What escaped my knowledge was the imminence of the naughtiness of CCAST Bambili students.

When a girl knew that a boy had fallen in love with her, she would attract the boy, then torment him for a long time before giving in. When a boy had his own chance too, he behaved likewise. This was a characteristic which was prevalent among students of this institution. Lesley might have had his chance. He must have discovered that I was madly in love with him and that I was completely docile. He was thus proving difficult. I however hoped that it wasn't deliberate.

'Don't also forget that you met me last 20th May Day on the way to our school and you told me yourself that you were in CCAST Bambili''. I was happy to have remembered this meeting in order to free myself from this rain of questions. But they kept on coming.

'OK. What is your problem with me?' This was a question I didn't like. It sounded familiar to me. I hesitated but it was not a time for kidding. 'Don't be timid. Tell him all' the inner voice said.

'I love you Lesley', another shot in the air.

'Why do you love me now?'

Why couldn't he be patient to let me talk? I wondered when those questions would cease.

'When you asked for my love, I was still a child. I had not known what it meant being in love. I wasn't yet mature enough to love. I later found that I couldn't love anyone else but you?'

'What makes you love me now?'

'Just nothing. It is natural'

'Are you sure that you are in love with me?'

'God knows that I am. Without you, I shall love no one else'

Lesley was silent. He seemed to be pondering on something. We were silent for about a minute. The sound of footsteps of patients was the only thing that disturbed this silence. Far in the other ward, 1 heard a rubber cup drop, might be from the hands of a weak and trembling patient. On the other side a nurse was reproaching a patient for having vomited medicine. I was in the students' ward in which two students shared each room. The girl in the next bed had been discharged just the morning before 1 came.

'Look at me, Ever!' Lesley broke the silence. 'If you were asked to recommend a girl for your younger brother, what would your choice look like?'

'I have never thought of it'.

'Try'

'I don't yet have a younger brother who is grown up enough to have a girl. Before he reaches that age, I would have thought'.

'I have one and would like that you advise me how to choose for him' he insisted. This was rather too difficult a question for me and I couldn't guess its importance. I thought for a moment.

'It would depend on the type of boy' I said.

'Give an example of a type of boy and the type of girl that suits him'

'But of what use is this question Lesley?'

'The future of our love' I again thought hard.

'My people believe that a slow and calm man should always look for a calm and boisterous woman and vice versus.' I told him. 'that is, one member should possess what the other hasn't for the sake of completion.'

'And what do you believe personally?'

'Not very different'

'Good, if I have understood you well, there should be contrast in their characters'

'Not in all cases,' I corrected.

'But in most of the cases'

'Yes'

'I have a younger sister who is wonderfully proud. She believes that she is the most beautiful girl in the world. She would never believe that she has a comparison. What type of man would you recommend for her?'

'I would choose a calm man for her for another proud man would constantly have friction with him. They would always argue about their different positions and would end up in a disaster'

'Well spoken Miss! I am a proud man'

'I don't understand you'

'I mean that I too, I am a proud boy, as proud as you'. I was still struggling to get the synthesis of this argument when the inevitable and indefensible bullet landed.

'Thank you for loving me now but I fear, I can't love you. Moreover, my love is already with someone else'.

I winced under the weight of this rebuff. No, it couldn't be so.

The trend of things was the wrong way. Why all this greed in love. I told him all.

'Please Lesley, I would die if you say so. I have been unable to love any other boy because of you. You have occupied my mind for all this time since I first met you. I have spent each day of the year searching for you. I have walked and carried you in my hands and in my dreams. Lesley dear, don't be so wicked'.

'The time is past'

'Please don't kill me. Take my hand and let us live forever'. I attempted grabbing his hand but he malevolently seized it away.

'Lady, I don't love anyone and if I were to love a girl, she would not be you'. The knife went straight into my heart at hearing my own words of two years back being quoted with its exact punctuation marks. The boomerang went home. I clutched at the bedposts not believing my ears at what I was hearing.

'Now I must take my leave Miss. See you next time'. He stood up and was walking away. At the door, he seemed to realize himself or he just wanted to insult me, I can't say. He came back; kissed me on my cheek and left.

Who has ever met such extreme situation in life? This kiss I had been dying to get had at last come but accompanied with the worst shock I ever had in life. What had Lesley actually said and what had he done? This was a puzzle. I did not know if to disbelieve my eyes or my ears.

Imagine a man who has won twenty million Francs in a lottery draw and learning at the same time that he has lost his newly married wife in a blazing inferno. Imagine a blind man gaining his eyesight and losing .his power to walk at the same time. Imagine a dog finally arresting a hare it has untiringly been chasing in the forest and at the same moment finding that one of its fore legs has been grabbed an iron trap. This is the type of situation in which I was. On one side, there was a sweet gentle and fragrant kiss. On the other, a boomerang from a long awaited sweetheart.

For about twenty minutes, maybe thirty, I was lost in thought and confusion. How would I behave if I met Lesley hack in the campus? While I bathed in this ocean of pell-mell, I was arrested by another hard knock on the door. The knock was hard and wild, a knock which I knew wouldn't come from any of the nurses. I trembled from the shock of this sound and told the knocker to come in. The door opened. The gateman entered showing a letter.

'Na you dem di call am say Evelyn Ndangeh Miss?' I

nodded surprised at where this letter could come from when I was not yet up to a day old in the ward. 'Some young man don give me this letter, talk say make me I find you quick quick give am for you. E talk say e go see you again for school.'

He handed the letter to me. All my three names appeared behind the letter in bold but roughly and hurriedly written prints. The handwriting didn't prove to be one I had ever seen before. I tore the letter open with shivering hands and immediately glanced at the bottom to see the sender. Impossible! I was again made to doubt my eyes. The letter read as follows.

Bamenda 10th December, 1975

Dear Ever,

It's true what people say. True love wanders on thorny paths. The sublime becomes absurd when exaggerated.

We've been on stage playing a comedy. We've been two actors, you one and I another. If it. has not taken effect, then of what avail has it been?

For two years, we have strangled and stricken love. For two years, we have learnt how to love the hard way. A physionomical analysis of low' has proved that it is incongruent to wantonness. Why shouldn't we exploit it now?

Let us now drop the bygones and present to the world a unique pair. Let us now act in prorata to the amorous constitution. Let the world draw samples from our eternal well. The birds of the woods shall one day sing. 'There was a couple that attempted to annihilate love. Love proved that it could rather annihilate the couple. They gave up the attempt and became one in sorrow, one in happiness and one in pain.

Be my Ever forever. Love and Kisses.

Lesley.

I had read so fast that I didn't understand it well. I went over it a second time, reading more slowly and pausing on certain ambiguous words, Lesley being very ambiguous in his nature. I digested both their surface and deep meanings.

The second reading was still unsatisfactory, and I had to go over a third and even a fourth time. It seemed a dream. I understood or thought I understood. All my pains disappeared instantly.

But take care, I thought. Was this another trap? Could it be that Lesley was luring me in order to blast me off after? The letter looked too earnest to be a bait. "Let the world draw samples from our eternal well', the letter had read.

The four days which I passed in the hospital dragged on like four years but like Hercules, I held on.

Chapter 9

Today is my fourth and last day in the hospital. Let us name it Day one. Lesley left me four days ago. This would be Day one because it shall be my first day in love with Lesley.

All through the night I haven't slept well. The few minutes I manage to sleep are squandered by nightmares. In one of them, I am struggling with Ramatou the wizard over Lesley. She holds one hand and claims ownership of him and I hold the other. Lesley only says, 'the better wins me'. There is a tug of war. I struggle and wake up.

I try to sleep again. Another nightmare. Lesley is in a boat alone in the Lake Barombi and I am standing on the shore. I beckon on him and he begins to paddle towards me. All of a sudden, he starts sinking. I beckon on him not to leave me behind. I scream and shout but the unmerciful lake devours him faster and faster. His struggles are to no avail. I scream louder and a nurse who happens to be passing by shakes me awake. I am very much ashamed.

'What's the matter?'

'Nothing, just a bad dream' I am relieved to see the nurse move off. For the rest of the night, I do no sleep.

The doctor is supposed to come at 9 o'clock and discharge me. At ten o'clock, I can be free to go back to Bambili. I am impatient I would have wished he comes at 7 a.m. At 8 a.m., the impatience mounts. I carry up myself and pack a few things into my hand bag. The nurse brings my breakfast but I cannot eat. 8.30. In thirty minutes, the doctor would be around. I plan to leave immediately after for the taxi park to take an early vehicle for Bambili. 9o'clock, the doctor isn't forthcoming. 9.30, 10 o'clock still no one. I look around if I can get a nurse to tell me what is happening but I can't get any. I am almost exploding with impatience. I prepare myself for any outcome.

A nurse rushes, past my window. She is so fast that I can't stop her. I realize that the other patients too have not been checked and are as worried as myself. Some of them have aggravated cases and are badly in need of the doctor. None of them is around to attend to them. 11 o'clock and even 12 o'clock still meet me in bed. No doctor or nurse.

I eavesdrop some patients conversing outside and I can only grab bits of it. Another fatal accident. Casualties are appalling. All the doctors and some of the nurses are engaged in attempting to seize some of the survivors from the ready fangs of death. My heart pounds fast and I quickly think of which of my relations could be journeying from Bafoussam. I can't think of any.

I learn that there has been a collision between an Exarcos tipper and a passenger bus and that seven persons have been butchered beyond recognition at the spot. Two have just passed away in the hospital in the morning and more deaths are still expected. I am annoyed at these drivers who run at very high speed and who know how devastating its consequences can be. It is because of the good roads, some say.

The doctor at last comes at 12.30 to make his morning visits. He apologizes and explains why he couldn't come early enough. 'First save the child who has fallen into fire before saving the one who has fallen in hot water'. I forgive him partially. He removes the bandages, gives the cut a last treatment and discharges me.

12 o'clock still meet me in bed, no doctor, no nurse.

I decide to rush straight to the park and get a cab for Bambili. In front of the men's ward, I see a crowd of people. Nurses are dragging patients up and down in stretchers. It does not interest me. Passing in front of the surgical ward, the crowd is even thicker. Victims of the accident of this morning are lying in there and some relations are around eagerly waiting for any developments. I still have no interest and wish to hurry back to school to meet my almighty.

I am already at the hospital Roundabout. I meet two second year students of CCAST Bambili hurrying to the hospital. We greet each other and they ask me.

'Did you go to see the CCAST student who has had an accident this morning?' One asks me.

"No, I was myself hospitalized. I don't even know that a CCAST student was involved'.

He is a second year student. Anyway, you might not know him: for he has not been in school since the whole of this term'.

'I hear his case is serious, that he is still in a coma' the second student says. I am not interested; I very much wish to hurry back to Bambili where my better side is probably waiting for me.

'Sorry, I can't accompany you people back to the hospital for I cannot walk well. I had an abscess which was incised four days ago and I have been in hospital since then.' They sympathize with my illness, wish me a quick recovery and continue to the hospital.

I reach the park and take a cab to Bambili. I reach there by 2 o'clock.

I decide to rush to the park to get a cab for Bambili.

Victims of the accident of this morning are lying and some relations are around waiting eagerly for any developments.

•

Chapter 10

In November and early December, the sun in Bamenda is hot. The whirlwinds are fiery at this time and can naked girls who are dressed in large flying gowns right to the navel. These winds are called the Harmattan. These winds are dry and have a characteristic of cracking lips. They render light skin dark and dark skin rough and whitish. They can change one from another climatic zone which is different to this to beyond recognition.

The Harmattan in Bambili is peculiar. This village is on a hill side. The winds fly over the valleys and beat themselves against this hillside.

I, being a patient was transformed almost beyond recognition. I looked rough and whitish and the Bambili-Bamenda road had done its own part in deforming me with its red dust. Some of my classmates had problems in recognizing me under the dust and I only had to introduce myself to them. Even Collette my most intimate friend was shocked when she saw how much I had emaciated. Without mincing her words she said I was ugly and that I needed special care to regain my beauty. Little did she know how tumultuous my days in the hospital had been.

The idea that I looked ugly disturbed me. There was one soul I didn't want to see me look ugly. I rushed to the lavatory and took a good bath. After, I dressed carefully in my jeans skirt and blue shirt and prepared to move to the boys' Hall to meet Lesley.

Collette had finally understood that I was in love with Lesley and our relations became very cordial again. But she herself had been as destitute of any news about Lesley as myself and it was only four days before, just the day I left the school for the hospital that she had seen Lesley. She had spoken with Lesley and Lesley had told her that he had gone to Britain for holidays and that he had written back to the school that he wouldn't come back to the Upper sixth; the reason why his name had not appeared on the list of Upper sixth students. Unfortunately he hadn't been able to get a school in Britain with his Ordinary level results to do computer sciences and had decided to return and complete school.'

'I told him you were ill and had gone to the hospital'. Collette told me.

'He overtook me at the three corners, no doubt, he told me that he too was going to the hospital',

'Really?

'True, he met me at the hospital and we had quite a good time'.

'Thus you really love him now?'

'I shall die with him'. I, of course .didn't tell her of the boomerang, neither of the letter which was well kept in my handbag, Collette was happy, wished us a good time. She told me that he was in the Independence Hall.

My heart was beating fast. I left to go out but returned to make a last look at my face mirror. I brushed off some intruding hair and put them in order, I moved out and as I looked at the Independence Hall, I shivered. What happens if I go and he refuses to receive me? I thought. I thought of taking along Collette who had long been an advocate of this union. Lesley wouldn't dare to behave naughtily in front of Collette. But why all this lack of courage? I stroke courage and went alone.

I shivered the more by the time I was approaching the

gate. There were four boys there in front of the gate looking directly into my face. My feet almost gave way. I managed to reach one of them and asked him Lesley's room. He showed me but doubted if he had returned from Bafoussam. I thanked him and passed into the hall.

This could not be clear to me. When could have Lesley gone to Bafoussam again and what for? I would be annoyed if I did not meet him. I searched for the door and found it, Room 8. I gave a light and feminine tap. No answer. It was already 4 o' clock and they couldn't still be sleeping. I knocked again and harder. A big voice, clearly not Lesley's answered.

'Yes, who?'

Without courage I pronounced my name in a low voice.

'Evelyn'

'Who?'

The person inside must have not recognized the voice or must have not heard at all.

'Evelyn' I spoke louder. The door opened and I greeted. 'May I know if Lesley is in? '

'No' the annoying response. 'He has not yet returned from Bafoussam'.

'What could have again taken him to Bafoussam at this time of the term?' I asked.

'You know he hasn't been here since the beginning of the term. He still had all his luggage and even books in Bafoussam. He went to get them four days ago. He also had to pass to the hospital, I don't know if he passed before going or he shall pass after' .

'He passed before going for 1 was in the hospital myself and he did not disclose to me that he would journey. When did he say he would come back to school?'

'He was supposed to journey .back today. Since tomorrow is a public holiday, he can just decide to spend the night **in** Bamenda and come back tomorrow.'

I thought fast. Would that day pass again without that I had seen Lesley? I needed him very badly. I had a fire burning in me to see him, a fire which could be extinguished by him alone. I had to hold him in my bands. I had bought some popcorn and some readymade groundnuts, a cake and some chocolate to give him. All of this was in my handbag ready for him. I could not store it any longer. I needed to give it to him that day. I made up my mind.

'Where does he spend the night in town I asked this boy who had been waiting for me to take my excuse and leave.

'Do you know the Alongeh Typing Institute at the Sonac Street at Ntamulung?' I nodded. 'Just directly behind it, there is another block house painted blue, with wooden windows. Ask for Mr. Nguepi's apartment. He is Lesley's uncle and it is with him that Lesley spends his nights in town.

'Thank you very much' I went out of the yard and crossed the yard into the road.

Chapter 11

It is 5 PM, still Day One. The sun is half way down the hill on its setting journey. Two ladies carrying a nkenja of sweet potatoes are coming back from the farm. A pig grunts and disappears into the grass behind me in its interminable search for food. A rat scampers across the road from the left to the right side. About thirty cattle egrets are crossing the village over us in search of a resting place for the night. A hawk flies amongst them but it is rather chasing a bird and putting out a forlorn cry. The wind is down but dust haze remains immobile in the air, dust which has been raised by vehicles on the dusty roads. Children can be heard screaming and clashing buckets as they draw water for the last time for the day.

I am again at the Bambili Three Comers waiting for a vehicle to take me to Bamenda. A Renault 12 comes and I fill the last empty seat. It is very old and can hardly go beyond 30 kilometers an hour. It still serves its purpose for I can't have any other choice. Before we are halfway the journey, the back tire fires. We get out and the driver takes not less than twenty minutes to replace it. The spare tire looks more miserable than the former. I boil with hate on these drivers who are more interested in extorting money from passengers than caring for their security.

We go slower in order to avoid the bumpy spots of the road. Before we reach Mile 4 Nkwen, another tire fires. It is already 7 p.m. there is no other spare tire. My hopes of reaching town and searching for Lesley's uncle's house are almost bleak. I must go. I can't do anything.

The driver keys his vehicle and tells us to pay him the

money so that he can go to a friend's house nearby and bring his vehicle to take us to town. We give him the money and he goes off. Ten minutes, twenty, fifty and one hour and he still does not come. Others insist that we wait for him. 8 p.m. already. I cannot wait. I start trekking.

I am daydreaming while walking. What can Lesley be doing now? What happens if I go to their house and meet him with a girl and a readymade program for the night? No. What happens if I reach there to find that he hasn't yet come back from Bafoussam? I would be done for; I don't know any responsible person in town with whom I can spend the night. I shouldn't think of such a thing.

I pray to meet him. We shall tell old tales. We shall talk about true love that wonders on thorny paths. I shall sing for him. I shall push him away if he attempts to hug me. We shall struggle. Then I shall take him in my hands and tell him that I am dying for him. Then I shall give him his cake and groundnuts. I shall put them in his mouth myself. He shall also try to feed me but I shall refuse at first, then shall accept. We shall eat with etiquette, drink with etiquette and might dance.

'Pem! Pem! Peeeem….!' A vehicle has narrowly missed me. I have been walking on the wrong side of the road and have wandered too far into the motorway. The driver throws insults at me.

'If you don chop flop, you no fit go die for bush?'
'Akwara!'

'When akwara dem don begin go for that dem market, dem no di run motor again?' Another thug who is coming from the opposite direction adds. Little do these sonofabitches know that I have not yet 'chopped' and that I am only striving for a start.

I take a cab at Mile 2 when I am already dead tired for my shoes are high-heeled and do not permit much trekking. The cab drops me at the Sonac Street and I have no difficulties in making out the Alongeh Typing Institute. I go behind the house as directed: I see the house and knock. A boy of about 14 opens. I greet and ask for Lesley. He looks confused.

'Has Lesley returned from Bafoussam?' he is more confused but answers.

'Yes'

'I mean Lesley went to Bafoussam, not so?' He nods doubtfully. 'He was supposed to return today, not so?' I am really bold now and I am dictating the pace of the conversation. On the contrary the boy is either timid or frightened by something I don't know.

'Which Lesley do you actually mean, sister?' The boy asks me with concern. 'I can't understand because...' I cut him with annoyance.

'I mean Lesley Njapa. Is this not where he stays when he comes town? I am from CCAST Bambili and I have an important message for him. My name is Evelyn Ndangeh' I know that this introduction is not necessary but cannot say why I have done it. It seems to have an effect on the boy.

'It would be better if you come tomorrow. You cannot see him today sister'.

'I very much wish to see him. I have a message for him which cannot wait. I earnestly beg you to tell me where he is. I can't sleep without seeing him. Please tell me'.

'He has gone out and shan't come back today. It is already too late to take you where he is. Maybe, if you come tomorrow, I can take you to him'.

'If your problem is the distance, I can pay the taxi fare, I have something to give him which would not still he valid by

77

tomorrow. I am appealing to you to dress up and lead me to where he is, be it in the hospital or in a party'.

'It is impossible sister' I am almost crying. Another tall man rushes by looking restless and in a haste. He brushes past me without even a word of greetings and disappears into the house. The boy follows him in. They speak in low tunes, then the man comes out and this time looks into my face and greets.

'Good evening Miss'

'Good evening Sir'

'I learn you wish to see Lesley'

'Yes'.

'Why don't you persevere and come tomorrow?'

'I have something for him which would lose its validity before tomorrow' I lie.

'By the way who are you?'

'My name is Evelyn Ndangeh. We are both students of CCAST Bambili'.

'Oh, you are Evelyn. He also intends to see you but not today; tomorrow perhaps'. This surprises me. So he had talked to his people about me. This rather increases my anxiety to see him.

'He shall be expecting you tomorrow.' He adds.

'Today is different from tomorrow. Why not just lead me to where he is if he actually is in town?'

'Do you really need to see him so badly? '

'Too badly' 1 quickly answer. They go in again and conspire for a few minutes. The man comes out and asks.

'If hake you to him, shall you really like to see him!'

'Be it in the devil's house, I shall see him'

OK, let us go' I am relieved.

Chapter 12

It was 10 PM still in DAY ONE. There was biting cold. The Sonac Street was very busy with people moving up and down. Some were in pairs and some were single. A few meters from us towards the church a woman was sitting over a basin of flour - baked cakes and a kerosene lamp on a chair near her lit a safe behind the basin. In the Modern Club Bar direction, a vehicle's lights lit some children engaged in a fight and a mob surrounding them. Dark figures of lovers dotted the sides of the streets, some pairs dragging each other and disputing on which direction to go.

I followed the man blindly not knowing where we were going to. He stopped a taxi and asked the driver to drop us at the Hospital Round about. I shivered but controlled my emotions. Why did he call Hospital Roundabout? Anyway, he had said it was at the roundabout and not at the hospital itself. I held my peace and the taxi dropped us there. He paid the fare and we started moving into the hospital compound. I was hopefully wishing that we branch off somewhere but he started making for the surgical ward.

'Where are we going to?' I asked frightened.

'Just come on. You wish to see Lesley, not so?'

'Yes', I answered without confidence.

We climbed the steps and entered the hospital building. I was no more talking, overcome by doubt and fear. Was Lesley assisting somebody in the hospital? He led me to the surgical ward. In front of one of the doors, I saw a crowd of people standing very mournfully. They were talking in low voices. Some seemed to have been crying, I held my heart. Was someone dead there and could it be Lesley. I followed on.

We started moving into the hospital compound

The man brushed the others aside and we entered. I saw a body placed in a bed. It was so deformed that I could not recognize it. The left side of the head was terribly swollen and covering the eye. The lips were wonderfully thick or swollen. There was a bandage round the head and it looked like the left ear was completely tom off for the bandage passed over it but the spot looked deprived of its property. I was confused.

I did not know who he was.

'Where is Lesley?' I asked the man.

'This is Lesley' he pointed at the body. He had a motor accident on his way from Bafoussam this morning. Has been in a coma since'.

For five seconds everything came to a standstill. Then the body turned with me for a few moments. I saw white red, blue and yellow, then a complete blackout.

I woke up many minutes after, in a bed I deduced to be the same I had left that morning of Day one. I was surrounded by a group of persons I could not immediately recognize all of them. The only thing that made me recognize the nurses was the white uniform they wore with the blue laces.

Like a cat surprised by a dog, I sprang up seized by fright. The nurses and the others fell on me and held me down: I did not know whether I had been dreaming or something had really happened,

'Where is Lesley? Lesley... Lesley... ?'

I shouted and struggled to free myself from the hands holding me. 'Leave me free, I wish to see Lesley, where is Lesley, let me go please Lesley, where are you?' I shouted and cried struggling hut the hands were unmerciful to me. 'Oh Lesley, come to me'.

In front of one of the doors, I saw a crowd of people standing mournfully. My heart missed a beat.

'Don't be silly', a voice very familiar to me scolded. "Who is Lesley? What have you in common with him?" I turned and looked at the face with some concern. My blood ran cold and I shrank in the bed surprised and ashamed at recognizing who he was. My father. My mother was there too, one of the nurses holding her hand.

I remember once, right back in the village, during a CYF come together, a riddle was posed if you arrived a scene and found your father and your husband trapped in a blazing inferno and you had the possibility to save only one of them, who would you save? To boys, father was replaced with mother and husband was replaced with wife.

I was overwhelmed by the answers some of my friends gave. Some of them said that if their husband and father were trapped in such an inferno; they would save their husband and let go their father. In better words, they preferred their husbands to their fathers.

At that time, I regarded such girls to be good for roasting or hanging, a good punishment for filial ingratitude. Asked why, they argued that with their husband or with their wife, they could produce many other fathers or wives but with their father or mother, they would not be able to produce any other being. The answer looked more unreasonable to me. I could not just imagine how I could neglect my dear father who brought me to the world, who gave me the paternal care when I was young and who had long been my protector, to choose somebody I had met only recently, who was none of my family members and to whom I owed no gratitude.

Day One was a D-Day for me. I had to give the correct answer to that riddle. I had to choose the right person and I hope you my reader would not doubt my choice.

Finding that I was calm and conscious, the nurses and the other persons I did not recognize took their leave and cautioned my parents not to be hard on me for I was mentally not very sound. They ceased bullying me. My father and mother drew the hospital stools near the bed and sat down. They offered a long prayer to God and my father told my mother to return to my uncle's house in the town and pass the night there, but she refused. Only when I pretended to be sleeping that he coaxed her to leave and she reluctantly left when it was almost past midnight, escorted into the taxi by one of the male nurses.

My father wore his old wind cheater and lay on the floor.

He soon fell.in a deep slumber leaving me free for my night
activities and that was the end of Day One.

The man brushed the others aside and we entered

Chapter 13

1.30 a.m. Day Two, my father who has journeyed all the way from the village is very tired and is snoring off on the floor. The lights are out in the wards and only dotted bulbs around the hospital compound are alive, I am alone in my ward as a patient and next to me is an empty bed. This is the same bed and the same ward in which I was when Lesley met me four days ago.

The hospital is half asleep. Only the nurses and the guards on night duty are awake. Each nurse has confined himself or herself into his/her ward and moves out or in only when occasion calls. An owl and a frog croak simultaneously for some moments and stop instantly, From the far end of the town, from the direction of Nkwen the CBC church bell chimes 1.30. I hear a patient groaning in the ward next to me. I think of Lesley. Dead or alive? I should know now. Here is my chance. I must seize it.

I raise myself up from bed. The bed creaks and my father stops snoring momentarily. I remain silent. Then he turns his head and leans the other side against the wall and continues snoring. I raise my legs from the bed and put them on the floor. Still no reaction from my father. I decide to do it barefoot. I tiptoe to the door. It has an inlock and its hinges are old and rusty. It must make noise. How do I manipulate it such that this alarming noise is drowned?

I press on the door lever. It makes a loud click. I hold my heart as my father stops snoring again but does not move. I again pull at the door. My father probably disturbed, sits up but does not care to look at the bed which is dark. I lean against the wall near the door, my heart in my hands and hardly breathing. My father gropes the floor for his bag, removes his sweater from it and wears it inside the overall then goes down prostrating on the floor. I wait until he starts snoring again.

I pull at the door tenderly. Click after click, it gets open just enough to squeeze myself out. I am tempted to leave it open for it would be another task to shut it. I wish to eliminate the least obstacle that would hinder me from achieving my aim. But no, the open door would let in cold which would wake up my father. If up, not seeing me would raise an alarm. It is better to close it. Again click after click, I pull the door shut.

There is a stony silence outside the ward. The hospital is as silent as a grave. There is biting cold outside and as I am not well armed against it, I am shivering. I tiptoe towards the male surgical ward, my heart beating hard. Just before I reach the corridor separating my ward from the next, I hear the footsteps of someone moving towards me from the far end of the building. Quickly I negotiate the corner into the dark corridor and crouch to avoid her. She moves unconcernedly and passes just about four meters from me, holding a syringe and a stethoscope. Her footsteps get lost at the other end of the building. I inspect the rest of the veranda and the path leading to the male surgical ward and finding it safe, I move out of my hiding place and move quickly to that direction. The sound of a Mercedes lorry dinning melancholically down the Mendankwe hill reaches me.

I move faster on the veranda. I skip into the path and pace it right to the male surgical ward. Before I step on the veranda, a door at the edge of the building opens abruptly and a running nurse out. With one leg already on the veranda, I kick myself back and on the lawn at the comer of the building in the darkness. The nurse races away from me towards the Pharmacy. I hear another patient groaning in that room. Another severe case, maybe.

I move fast towards Lesley's room. I notice the door.

The nurse races away from me towards the pharmacy

• The crowd is no more there. It might be he is already dead and carried back home, maybe transferred to the mortuary. My heart pounces fast and I move faster. I will die if he is not there. I wish it were a dream.

I reach the door and peep through the window. The room is lighted but silent. I go nearer shivering, my legs almost giving way. I see the body, the same one I thought I saw in a dream and maybe still in. dream, not a dream. This time I am very conscious, and this time, the body does not turn with me. I compose myself and study it courageously. It is breathing for I see the chest moving up and down. The bandages are still there. Translucent tubes are connected to his body and taped at various parts. The body is not moving. The only eye lean see, for the other one has disappeared in the swollen head is closed.

I see Lesley's face in the body, Lesley's serene face, Lesley's real self. Lesley's words sing in my mind.

"Let the world draw samples from our eternal well. The birds of the woods shall one day sing. There was a couple that attempted to annihilate love. Love proved that it could rather annihilate the couple. They gave up the attempt and became one in sorrow, one in happiness md one in pain". Here we are, in sorrows and in pain, thus, we need to be one. A rage seizes me and I plunge at the door and blow it open. The body does not move, nor is there any sound from any other place. I close the door behind me not caring about how much sound it makes move to the bed.

The rate of breathing is a little bit too fast, in fact, panting, I am tempted to kiss it, my second kiss in life. I withhold myself. It should be done with his consent. I raise my hand to shake him awake.

I hear footsteps on the veranda moving towards me. I am confused of what to do. If I move out, I shall surely meet him on the veranda. If I remain in and if it happens that the person is coming in this ward, he shall meet me in. I am surely caught this time. I am confused. The person moves to the door and I think fast. I study the single person ward. There is a wardrobe on one side and a cupboard on the other, no toilet room. The wardrobe is half closed by a blue blind and in it, two dirty costumes and a towel are on a hanger. Before the person outside can tum on the lever, I dive into the wardrobe which is just large enough to contain me and draw closed the blind.

A nurse and a doctor come in.

'Still in a coma' says the nurse.

'How many bottles of drips have you used?' the doctor asks.

'This is the fifth since morning. You know he lost quite a good quantity of blood. He needs much of this'.

'Exactly, looks like the rate of breathing has improved much'

'Yes'

'And what about his body temperature?'

'Has improved too'

The doctor raises the white sheet covering Lesley. I notice too that the whole of his chest is plastered. Despite this plaster, there is still much bleeding as almost a third of it is wet. The doctor examines it but covers it. Contrary to my fears, the doctor says

'The bleeding has stopped'.

'Since some hours ago' confirms the nurse.

'That bottle of glucose is almost empty. Do you still have any left?

'Two'

'Right, fit that now, and study him closely then'

'Understood doctor'

The doctor moves out leaving the nurse. I pray that he does not open the wardrobe. He lifts up Lesley's head, then places it well. He is not better than a corpse. Then the nurse goes to the cupboard, opens it and takes out a bottle of drip goes to the stand against the wall and fits it to the tube.

After, he goes' to the tap and washes his hands, then moves towards me, maybe to get the towel to wipe his hands with. Just when he sends his hands to draw the blind open and to expose me, the doctor blows the door open calling on him. He hesitates.

'I almost forgot' the doctor speaks. 'What has happened with the girl who fell unconscious in this room after seeing this patient?'

'You mean the girl with the cerebral malaria I guess?'

'Yes. How is her condition?

'I hear after taking the sedative, she had a good sleep and awoke greatly improved and calm'. It looks like she's got something doing with this patient.

'I do think so too. They come from the same institution and you know the rate of moral decadence of that institution.'

'And which is that institution?'

'CCAST Bambili'

'Oh, is it that school that went on a strike for sex?

'Exactly, the higher secondary school which calls itself a campus'.

'This her illness is amorous and can be very dangerous for these juveniles especially patients of cerebral malaria'

'I must assure you doctor, our schools are breeding wonders these days' the nurse speaks wiping his hands on his apron forgetting that he was coming to open the blind to get a towel for that purpose.

'In what ward is she?' the doctor asks.

'The special ward'

'I will visit her'. The doctor moves out. The nurse arranges a few things in the cupboard and moves out too closing the door behind him.

They are surely going to raise an alarm if they do not find me in bed. My father in particular and the night watchman would be held responsible. I move out of my hideout and decide to take another course to run to my ward before the doctor gets there. No, but this is Lesley in pain. and in sorrow by me, why leave him alone?

I move nearer him. There is a stench like the one I smell in the butchery.

'Lesley ... Lesley' I call. No answer, no movement. 'Lesley, Lesley... this is Evelyn, your only one, in life and in death, in sorrow and in pain please answer me, speak to me, Lesley', still no answer, no movement. I go again nearer, bend over him and give him a tender kiss. Then I call again, 'Lesley dear, you are leaving me to who? You are a mockery of my efforts, you are a mockery of the only one who loves you and who shall still love you'.

His head turns and the whole bed shakes. The newly fitted bottle of drips goes down splashing on the cement floor and bits of glass scatter carelessly on it.

It looks like my eyes have deceived me or it is a reality. Did his hand really move? I call again, 'Lesley'. I see the two legs fold and stretch out again. Then his head turns and the whole bed shakes. The newly fitted bottle of drips goes down splashing on the cement floor and bits of glass scatter carelessly on it. Just at that moment, the doctor, the nurse and my father come running.

'Here she is, the mad girl' the nurse shouts running in. 'She has displaced the patient and has pulled down the bottle and broken it on the floor. Hold her'

The three of them pounce on me, raise me high and carry me out with deadly grips.

'Leave me free' I shout 'I am not mad, I am conscious of what I am doing. Lesley is not in a coma any more. He is moving. Let me talk to him'. I struggle and beat the nurse to leave me free but his grip in particular is unmerciful.

They take me back to my ward, chain my legs and hands to my bed. Then they give me another narcotic injection amidst shouting.

'I am not mad. I am not off senses", I cry.

'A mad person never knows that he is mad', the wicked nurse says. The rest of that night and the whole day; I am in chains.

News goes to the village and to my school that I am fully mentally deranged and that I am very boisterous in the hospital. My friends and relations come to see me and everything I say is dismissed for foolishness. My mother sits near my bed crying the whole day. Surprisingly I learn that Lesley is still in a coma and that all the displacements have been caused by me.

That day passes away for both of us miserably and that is the end of Day Two.

Chapter 14

In the morning of Day three Collette arrived the hospital at about 7 a.m. accompanied by some friends. Collette too had learnt that I was mentally deranged and was terribly shocked with the news.

She was the only one I was waiting for to save me from this asylum of a ward. She was the only one who knew the secret between me and Lesley and would be the only one to understand me.

I was thus waiting for her to convince her to vindicate me. When she was arriving, a nurse was escorting me to the toilet, my hands chained to one of my legs. When I saw her, I ran to fall on her and to embrace her. She was frightened and avoided me and was actually escaping from me.

The nurse ran after me and caught me by the chains. 'Take care of her', the nurse warned Collette. 'She is dangerous when loose'

'Oh Collette dear', I complained. 'All believe that I am insane. There is nothing wrong upstairs please. Only something those who are not concerned cannot understand'. Collette only looked shocked at the gravity of my insanity as the nurse drew me to the toilet by the chains.

When we returned to the ward, Collette followed us and watched me chained to my bed.

'Why do you have to chain her?' Collette asked the nurse. 'She is very dangerous when loose. She strays around and sometimes goes into the male surgical ward. 'The night before last, she entered the male surgical ward and turned a certain patient who is in a coma up and down despite the delicateness and fragility of this patient.

After this, she pulled down the bottle of drips the patient was using and dashed it onto the floor. Luckily we came in time to save the patient, else she would have killed him'.

Collette and her friends were spellbound at learning of this vandalistic action of mine. My case was surely grave, one of them commented.

'I am her nearest friend and classmate from secondary school and both of us are now in Bambili. 1 would like to converse with her secretly if you could excuse us' Collette told the nurse.

'She talks nothing but rubbish', the nurse protested. 'Anyway, if you insist on hearing some of her babbling, I will leave you to do so', she left but warned. 'Only take care that she doesn't harm any of you for she can be very dangerous'.

'We will take care of that sir', Collette promised.

The nurse left us and I was relieved. My father too left.

'I am not insane as people believe. Listen to me carefully. I shall explain to you in detail and I shall prove to you that I am very sane and conscious of everything that I have been doing. I am not abnormal in any way'

'That is not true, Evelyn. A normal person cannot wander about in the night as to go as far as entering the male surgical ward to displace tender bodies and dislocate surgical installations'

'Dear Collette, listen to me let me clarify you'. I sat up and drew the chains and Collette and her friends shook and shifted back with fright.

'Take care' the other warned. 'Don't go too near her, she can pounce at any time without warning.'

'No my friend' I cried. 'I am not mentally demented. I am nor wild. Ask me everything we have been doing Collette, and I shall give you the correct answers'

'Let us converse on any familiar topic and you shall prove whether I am abnormal or not?' The other mate laughed and clapped her hands.

'This reminds me of my uncle' she said, 'When he has filled himself up with alcohol to the brim and when he is gay he argues that he has not taken a thing and that he is more reasonable than all of us'. All of them giggled.

'But that is not the same case with me friends, I am as normal as a summer day'. They laughed the more and a passing patient halted to study my lunatic behavior. I waved her away but she hesitated.

Then I drew the chains and they rattled as though they were loose and the patient fled for life.

'Now Evelyn, if you say you are actually sane, tell me exactly what happened from the day you left me in Bambili to Lesley's hall, the boy's Hall until how you found yourself here and in this mess?

You didn't tell me you were to go to Bamenda after that. You are still wearing the same dress you wore yesterday. You seem not to have changed any inner wears which isn't normal of a girl of your standard'.

'I understand you perfectly well Collette and you shall be convinced when I finish my story'.

Then I told her all, narrating every detail which could prove my point. I told her about the boy in the boy's Hall who directed me, Lesley's mate, about our miserable journey to town, about Lesley's uncle and our trip to the hospital.

All three of them listened with interest and concern, hardly believing that it was me talking, me a mad girl. I spoke and spoke and each time the chain rustled, they kept their distance. What I could not narrate in detail was what happened after I arrived and discovered Lesley in a coma.

'Maybe I fainted or something happened which I could not explain', I told them. 'However, what I can remember is that I woke up in the same bed I left that morning surrounded by people I did not know.

What I wanted to know was Lesley's situation, and it could be that, it was the cause of my boisterous behavior in bed that night until I discovered that my parents were present'.

Collette was looking convinced and I seized the opportunity to be fluent in my narration. I told her about Lesley's letter and recited it from the beginning to the end. It sounded genuine to them. We were to be one in pain, the reason why I abandoned my father in my ward and moved to the surgical ward that day.

I explained all what happened there. 'I didn't raise my hand to touch Lesley but for the kiss I gave him. He moved, I told them but this sounded very unbelievable to them. A man in a coma cannot move just at calling his name and if at all he moves, he cannot go back to it after. I swore to them that he did and could still do it even though he was still in a coma as they believed.

There was disbelief on their faces. 'Lesley is not in a coma. He is only broken down and is suffering from a deep sleep', I assured them.

They believed the first part of the story but doubted the second. To prove to them that I was not finished, I narrated to them all what happened in school, what was happening then and what plans the school had for the immediate future.

'A mad man is always very informed', this girl who I was beginning to hate commented. I ignored her and sent them to go to Lesley's ward and ask everything I had said from his uncle about that night. If he spoke differently, they could know that I· was really insane. They readily went and asked him and he confirmed my story of that night. They were beginning to get convinced that I was not mentally abnormal. They too were seeing Lesley's horrific state for the first time and wailed.

They called for the doctor to come and hear my testimony. He came and I told him all, speaking courageously of my love with Lesley, the reason why I stole to his ward that night. They called Lesley's uncle and he came and confirmed that Lesley had spoken to them about me. My father came to hear me and the doctor told him all for I had not the heart to tell him about my lover or fiancé as the doctor put it.

'Lesley is no more in a coma;'1 told them. 'He is only sleeping deep and could be awakened if we care to. Just let me do it without touching him after all, it would cause no harm'. They did not believe that. When we were talking, our parish pastor who had learnt of the sad news came to offer prayers. He studied everything I said carefully. Then told the audience in the ward, 'All of you listen to me; God, the supreme and the creator of everything is exceptional in everything he does. He can do and undo. We do not know what powers he has given this child to cure. Let us not argue her much. As she says she can put up this patient from his death steep, let us permit her try it. If she says the man is hers, let us give him to her. She has knocked, let it be opened to her as the book of God cautions. Jesus Christ did miracles through the power of God: It maybe this is another power he has given this child to perform us a miracle'.

Everyone agreed and the chains were released from my hands and legs. Then the congregation moved to the male surgical ward. The nurse moved next to me making sure that

I did not make a surprise skip. We entered the room in which Lesley was sleeping unendingly. Everyone was silent when we entered. A bottle of drip was still hanging over him. I ordered the doctor to disconnect it and he did. Then I moved near the bed and called.

'Lesley ... Lesley my love, your only one in life and who shall be in death is by you. Lesley my darling, Lesley my heart, wake up, and talk to me. Lesley my angel, this is Evelyn talking. Please, wake up and talk to me. If ever you have loved Ever, wake up and talk to her now.'

The right hand lifted itself to the stomach and the head turned. The nurse retreated right to the door scared by what he was seeing. I continued invoking, quoting some phrases of his letter. Soon his legs moved, then the whole body turned and rolled from front to back and from back to front. Then he yawned and uttered a scraggy sound. 'The doctor, the pastor, my father and Lesley's uncle looked in disbelief but no one uttered a word. Out of a sudden, he started calling, his eyes still closed.

'Evelyn ... Evelyn…'

'Here is Evelyn' I answered. 'This is Evelyn herself talking to you'. I gave him my hand and he held it and opened his only eye for the other one was sealed. The eye moved from me to his uncle and to the others and he called.

'Uncle, take care of Evelyn, be good to her' then he turned to me and said, 'Evelyn my love, I have been unable to die because of you.

His voice was dry and tough and that his only eye looked languid he continued, 'but the gratitude and the love I owe to you has sent me back. I didn't want to be a mockery of your love. If I could live, I would live for you alone and the birds of the woods would sing of our true love.'

'I have gone many times. But you see yourself that I cannot live. If I am still talking and breathing, it is for the sake of your love for inside me there is nothing left. I have no body now. I only have the soul which shall be yours for time on end. Then he turned again and groaned. 'I see someone with you like a pastor, am I right?'

'Yes' I answered.

'Bring him, let him unite us'. The pastor moved nearer the bed. He took my hand and put it over Lesley's and then prayed. At the end, I felt like I was lighter, like a new life had been given to me. The air smelt sweeter and I felt like a heavy load had been lifted off my body.

Then Lesley spoke after the prayers.

'Uncle, tell the world to be kind to Evelyn, 1 love her. Then he turned to me and said 'Evelyn, I am still yours till days unend'

When he finished, he turned away his head. The movements ceased and the rate of breathing multiplied.

The one eye went duller and the breathing culminated into one hard breath and ceased. The eye remained still and that was the end. Like a candle, his flame was out and like a dream the curtain was drawn on him. Further and further he was going and never to come back. He was already in the land of the unknown and with him he carried his words, the words which were never to be heard again.

I was petrified for some minutes, then was escorted out by the pastor and Lesley's uncle. At the veranda, I met the stretcher and at the path, I met the hearse and that was the end of Day Three and the end of the tale.

Epilogue

*T*here is a spot about one hundred meters south of the Ntamulung Church which I visit again and again each year. When the November dragonflies flutter in the air welcoming the Harmattan, when the plants are flowering and when lovers gather together to make plans for the end of year festivities, I visit this spot.

When in July the winds are fiery, breaking down houses and it is raining cats and dogs, when chicks seek for protection by clustering together under their mother and lovers cling in a warm embrace, I visit this spot.

Here lies my happiness and joy. Here lies my sadness and sorrows. It is a mound of red earth ovally surrounded by black stones. On the western end of it is a wooden cross bearing the following inscription with white paint.

Lesley Njapa. Born 1953. Died 1975
R.I.P